FICTION
Bai

Bailey, Linda.

Seven dead pirates

DUE DATE   **BRODART 09/15**   16.99

TWEEN FICTION BA

Seven Dead Pirates

A GHOST STORY BY
LINDA BAILEY

TUNDRA BOOKS

Tundra Books, a division of Random House of Canada Limited,
a Penguin Random House Company

Library and Archives Canada Cataloguing in Publication

Bailey, Linda, 1948-, author
Seven dead pirates / by Linda Bailey.

Issued in print and electronic formats.
ISBN 978-1-77049-815-0 (bound).—ISBN 978-1-77049-817-4 (epub)

I. Title.

PS8553.A3644S49 2015   jC813'.54   C2014-906939-1
                                                  C2014-906940-5

Published simultaneously in the United States of America by
Tundra Books of Northern New York,
a division of Random House of Canada Limited,
a Penguin Random House Company

Library of Congress Control Number: 2014952940

Edited by Tara Walker
Designed by Terri Nimmo
The artwork in this book was rendered in traditional pen and ink.
The text was set in Century Schoolbook.
Printed and bound in the USA

Tundra Books,
a division of Random House of Canada Limited,
a Penguin Random House Company
www.penguinrandomhouse.ca

1 2 3 4 5   19 18 17 16 15

TUNDRA BOOKS | Penguin
               Random
               House

For Maurice

It was the worst birthday party Lewis had ever been to. But then, what could you expect when the guest of honor was a corpse?

Okay, so Great-Granddad wasn't *exactly* a corpse. But he sure looked like one. The old man lay stiff on his back on the narrow bed. His eyes stared sightlessly, and his mouth was fixed open in a round toothless O. If it weren't for the pink party hat, you'd never guess he was alive.

Party hats! At a 101st birthday party. It was ridiculous. Lewis's parents certainly looked ridiculous, with their dark-rimmed glasses and pointy cardboard heads. He, Lewis, must look ridiculous, too, in the clown hat Mrs. Binchy had forced on him. As for Mrs. Binchy, she was the silliest of all, wearing a gold paper crown as she bustled in with the cake.

When Lewis's father spotted the cake, his eyes darted nervously around the room. Lewis knew what he was looking for. A fire extinguisher! The cake was ablaze with candles, and a draft from the window was fanning them into a bonfire.

"I couldn't do 101 candles, of course," said Mrs. Binchy breathlessly. "That would be foolish. But I wanted to do at least half, and I think I managed. Mr. Douglas, look! We've brought you a lovely cake. All together, everyone. *Happy birthday to youuuu . . .*"

Lewis's parents joined in, his mother's powerful voice drowning out the others. Seeing Lewis hesitate, she frowned. Lewis sang.

"Happy birthday, Great-Granddad. Happy birthday to you!"

Mrs. Binchy smiled and motioned for Lewis to take Great-Granddad's place blowing out the candles. It took three tries.

"I *do* love a party!" said Mrs. Binchy.

The whole thing had been her idea. Mrs. Binchy was Great-Granddad's housekeeper, and Lewis figured the party was just an excuse for her to have company. She must get lonely, living in a sprawling old house like Shornoway with nobody but Great-Granddad to talk to.

"Just imagine!" Mrs. Binchy was saying. "A hundred and one years old! I hope I look half that good when I'm his age."

Beaming, she passed around slices of chocolate cake. Lewis cheered up as he reached for his piece—a three-layered beauty, with marshmallow frosting and chocolate shavings on top.

He dug in, trying to remember the last time he'd had birthday cake. When he was little, he'd gone to parties where the whole class was invited, but now that his classmates were older, they only invited their friends. Lewis mostly celebrated birthdays with his family, which was small—just him, his parents and his father's sister, Aunt Edith in Boston. And Great-Granddad, of course. Lewis stared at the scrawny figure under the sheets, wondering whether he might not enjoy a piece of his own cake. He would have, in the old days.

When Great-Granddad was younger—ninety-five or ninety-six—he'd been a whole different person. He'd called Lewis "Sonny Boy" and slipped him crumpled twenty dollar bills when his parents weren't looking. He'd made jokes that only Lewis appreciated, sticking straws up his nose and making walrus noises.

And, once in a while, he had yelled at people who weren't there.

"Leave me be, you waterlogged old bludger!" Great-Granddad would holler, glaring into an empty corner of the parlor.

Or he might shake a fist at the peeling wallpaper. "I've no time for your foolishness! Can't you see I have visitors?"

Lewis thought the yelling was funny. But his mother just sighed. *She* thought Great-Granddad was crazy. Not that she ever used that word. Dementia was what she called it. Lewis knew what that meant. Nuts. Bonkers. Loony.

"More cake, Lewis?" said Mrs. Binchy. "I'm sure *you* still have room." She cut a thick wedge.

As quickly as Lewis held out his plate, his mother intercepted. "Thank you, Mrs. Binchy. I think not."

Mrs. Binchy's gray curls bobbed in surprise. "But surely on this special occasion . . ."

"Sugar disagrees with Lewis."

Lewis clenched his teeth. It wasn't *sugar* he disagreed with. He and *sugar* got along just fine, thank you.

He waited, quiet and cake-less, hoping Mrs. Binchy would argue. And she might have, except that Lewis's mother began peppering her with questions about

4

Great-Granddad. His medications. His blood pressure. Even his—ugh!—bowel movements.

Slumping in his chair, Lewis began to poke at the stuffing escaping from its arm. The furniture in Shornoway was falling apart, just like the old house itself.

"Pssst!" said Great-Granddad.

Lewis blinked, then stared at the bed. Great-Granddad's face on his pillow looked exactly the same, but his left hand had risen slightly off the yellowing sheet, and his pointer finger stuck out.

As Lewis watched, the O-shaped mouth moved. "Sonny Boy!" it whispered. The finger beckoned.

Lewis glanced around.

His father was dozing, and his mother and Mrs. Binchy were talking about bedsores. So no one heard Great-Granddad. No one except Lewis, who stared again at the clawlike finger, hooked and gesturing. Holding his breath, Lewis rose to his feet.

"Closer!" whispered Great-Granddad in a voice as thin as tissue paper.

Lewis swallowed hard and obeyed. He leaned his head toward the old man's, expecting something awful—foul breath, at the least. But all he could smell was a medicinal odor, like cough drops, and the general mustiness of the room.

"Libertalia," rasped Great-Granddad with difficulty. Then, more urgently, *"You!"*

Lewis watched as the mouth slowly returned to its O. The finger relaxed.

Libertalia?

Lewis waited politely. He cleared his throat. "I beg your pardon?" he said to Great-Granddad.

"Lewis?" His mother's voice. "Is Granddad all right? Did he speak?"

Lewis nodded.

"What did he say?"

Lewis didn't answer. He stared at Great-Granddad, transfixed.

"Well?"

Lewis wasn't sure why he didn't tell her. It wasn't like him to lie, not even a white lie. Maybe it was his second piece of cake, still sitting there, uneaten. He heard himself say, "I don't know."

Mrs. Binchy gave Great-Granddad a pat. "His teeth are out, poor dear. You can't understand a word."

"It would be nonsense, anyway," said Lewis's mother.

Nonsense, thought Lewis. Was that what it was?

Later, as they drove home, his parents had the conversation they always had after visiting Shornoway. Mrs. Dearborn said it was high time Great-Granddad was moved out of that drafty old wreck of a house. He should be in a hospital for the elderly where he could get professional care. Mr. Dearborn replied that yes, the situation was awful, but at least Mrs. Binchy was a kind soul. They both agreed there was nothing they could do. Great-Granddad had given instructions to his lawyer that he was not to be moved from Shornoway unless his doctor decided it was necessary.

Lewis didn't say anything, but he for one was glad Great-Granddad still lived at home. Even if it was wrecked and shabby, even if it smelled funny, it was better than visiting a hospital. And after all, Shornoway *had* been a grand mansion once, a long time ago when it was first built. Even now, with most of the rooms closed off, you could still feel *something* as you walked down the halls. A cool, prickly pulse of long-gone excitement. Sometimes it was so strong it made the hair on Lewis's arms stand up.

And sitting now in the back seat, Lewis wondered, as he'd wondered since he'd first heard them, about Great-Granddad's whispered words.

Libertalia. Had he gotten it wrong? No. He was sure that was what the old man had said. But what did it mean? And why did he say "you"? With such insistence, as if giving Lewis an order?

It probably *was* just nonsense, as his mother had said. All the same, Lewis decided to look up *libertalia* when he got home.

He fell asleep instead. His father led him, dozy, into the house.

The next morning, when his mother woke him to say that Great-Granddad had died in the night, Lewis was struck by an ache so powerful it took his breath away. It was like a fist clenching in his chest—and it surprised him. After all, they had been expecting this for a long time. Waiting, even.

He reminded himself that Great-Granddad was extremely old. He told himself that it couldn't be much fun, lying on your back that way, staring at the ceiling, while other people gobbled up your chocolate-marshmallow cake.

Still, the ache remained.

Then he remembered. *Libertalia. You!*

"Did he say anything?" asked Lewis. "You know. Before . . ."

"He died peacefully in his sleep, Lewis. He hasn't said anything sensible in weeks."

As the door closed behind her, Lewis shook his head. His mother was wrong. Great-Granddad *had* spoken. To him, Lewis. To him, alone!

At that, the tension in his chest eased. Lewis would

never have said it out loud, but the thing he suddenly felt was . . . proud. Of all the people in the whole world, Great-Granddad had chosen *him* to say his last words to.

And he knew suddenly, with a pounding in his heart, that those words had not been nonsense. They couldn't be. Not the last words of a man who had lived so long and done so much. The very last words! They had to mean *something*.

Libertalia. You!

He asked his parents the next day. What does it mean? *Libertalia*. Neither of them knew. His father checked a dictionary, but it wasn't listed.

"Sounds like the name of a rock-and-roll band," said Mr. Dearborn. "Heh, heh. Why don't we look on my computer?"

They did a search, but the results were confusing. There was a game called Libertalia, and there was also a long-ago place called Libertalia that may or may not have been real.

"A pirate haven," said Mr. Dearborn, reading aloud. "It was mentioned in a book written in 1724 called *A General History of the Pyrates*. Supposed to be . . .

let's see . . . a kind of perfect society. A place where pirates could live as equals, in peace and harmony. Heh, heh. Funny idea, that. Pirates living in harmony? Says here that this Libertalia was on Madagascar. That's an island, Lewis, just off Africa."

"I know," said Lewis. "So what do you think, Dad? Did Libertalia really exist?"

Mr. Dearborn shook his head. "I don't think so." He leaned forward to squint at the computer screen. "No proof of any kind. Just a legend. Good bit of fun, though! I remember, I used to play pirates when I was your age."

No, thought Lewis. Not when you were *my* age. Nobody plays pirates when they're almost twelve.

But he nodded and said, "Thanks, Dad."

Lewis's parents were ancient as parents go, so Mr. Dearborn had not been twelve for a *very* long time. He'd forgotten what it was like. He had also become a historian, which meant that he didn't believe anything that didn't come out of a book or museum.

As Lewis wandered away, he was more confused than ever. *Libertalia.* He couldn't stop thinking about it.

He repeated the strange word to himself, like a chant, through Great-Granddad's funeral. Which turned out to be nothing like he'd expected. For one thing, hardly anyone came. Aside from his family and Mrs. Binchy, there were just four people there, all old. Two women, one man and one he-wasn't-sure. Nobody cried except Mrs. Binchy, who snuffled noisily into a ratty tissue. Lewis wondered if *he* was supposed to cry. He couldn't. Not if he'd tried. The service seemed to be about a stranger—some guy who had once been chairman of the Library Building Committee.

"What?" whispered Lewis's mother. "What did you say?"

"Nothing," said Lewis. *Libertalia.* He must have been saying it out loud.

"Yes, you did. You were mumbling again."

Lewis pressed his lips together.

"Stop mumbling," said his mother.

The next morning, when his parents went to see Great-Granddad's lawyer about the will, Lewis asked to go along. Maybe there'd be a clue, something to explain those last words.

The lawyer's name—Mr. Lister—might have made Lewis laugh if he hadn't coughed hard instead. He recognized Mr. Lister as one of the old people from the funeral. A tiny man, he looked even smaller sitting behind his huge desk, surrounded by dusty files. He read the will aloud in a sandpaper voice. Lewis didn't pay much attention until he heard his mother gasp.

"Surely you can't be serious!"

"Yes, indeed," rasped the lawyer. "Those are the terms of the will, Mrs. Dearborn. You inherit everything—the house known as Shornoway, all the property including the beachfront and all the furnishings. But your grandfather *did*, as I say, place a condition. Before you can inherit, your family— meaning yourself, Mr. Dearborn and young Lewis here—must live in the house called Shornoway for a period of at least six months."

Mrs. Dearborn's broad, pale face went as white as paper. "*Live* in Shornoway? That crumbling horror? Have you *seen* Shornoway?"

"Oh my, yes." Mr. Lister broke into a wheezing chuckle. "But Mr. Douglas had strong feelings about the property, and I imagine he hoped . . . well, in any case, the will is clear. And quite in order. "

"In order" meant there was nothing to be done. Mrs. Dearborn argued for half an hour, just to make sure. If the Dearborn family wanted to inherit Shornoway, they would have to go *live* there. If they refused, the property would go to the Benevolent Association for Sailors Lost at Sea.

"There's just one other small bequest in the will," said Mr. Lister. "For Lewis."

Everyone stared at Lewis. He sank deeper into his big leather chair.

The lawyer read aloud. "To my great-grandson, Lewis, I leave my ship in a bottle. He will find it in the tower room of Shornoway. The key is in Mrs. Binchy's possession."

There was a long silence.

"That's *it*?" said Mrs. Dearborn.

The lawyer nodded.

"A ship in a bottle? A *bottle*? Lewis! Do you know anything about this?"

Lewis shook his head.

"However that may be," said Mr. Lister, "that is Mr. Douglas's entire will. Please let me know what you decide."

Mrs. Dearborn was not happy as they left the lawyer's office. For days, she was in what Lewis's father called "a state." Even though the Dearborns' house was nothing special—in fact, it was pretty much identical to every other house on Maplegrove Crescent—she hated to be forced to move. And the list of things she disliked about Shornoway grew longer every hour. The damp. The dirt. The rot. The drafts. The mold. The spiders. The mice. And worst of all, the stairs, which would be "utterly impossible," she said, for her arthritic knees.

Mr. Dearborn did his best to soothe her. He pointed out that Lewis could stay in his same school. He reminded her that oceanfront property was worth quite a lot of money. And six months wasn't, after all, such a long time.

"It might not be so bad," he said. "Perhaps we could even use a change?"

The look Mrs. Dearborn gave him after *that* remark sent him scurrying to his study.

In the end, she decided to do it—move the family to Shornoway. And then everything happened quickly. A FOR RENT sign appeared on the lawn of Lewis's house. Moving men were hired, and the Dearborn family was thrown into packing.

Nobody asked Lewis how *he* felt about moving. If they had, he would have had trouble answering. He had always liked visiting Shornoway, and there was that strange something about the house that he couldn't explain—that tingle of excitement in the air. Unlike his mother, he didn't mind the mouse droppings or the spiders. And he loved the beach.

But it would be, as his father said, a change. Lewis wasn't sure how he felt about a change as big as Shornoway. He had enough to deal with right now. Summer was almost over. In less than two weeks, school would begin.

The moment that thought entered his brain, he shut it out. He reminded himself not to think about *that.*

Not yet.

Not until he had to.

3

The Dearborns drove to Shornoway ahead of the moving van. As they crunched down the gravel driveway, Lewis leaned forward to catch a first glimpse.

It was a house to feel sorry for, he thought, like an old beggar lady who used to be beautiful. It stood tall against the bright summer sky, but the white paint was peeling badly, and gray wood showed beneath. Two windows were boarded over, while others gaped blindly between sagging shutters. Thistles choked the knee-high grass.

The car stopped. Lewis looked up. There! The tower room, where his ship in a bottle would be. The room faced the sea, so Lewis could see only the back of it from here. But he'd gazed up so often from the beach that he knew exactly what it looked like—round, with three tall windows and a pointed roof. Like a castle tower! As for the inside . . . well, he'd never actually *been* inside the tower. The top floor of Shornoway, too expensive to heat, had been shut off for years.

The front door banged open. Out burst Mrs. Binchy, red-faced and clutching a broom.

"Here already? Just let me get a few of these cobwebs." She whacked her broom enthusiastically into a dusty corner. "There now! Come in. Sorry for my appearance, Mrs. Dearborn. I meant to change. Where does the time go?"

The housekeeper brushed at a sagging skirt that might have been blue once, but was now a dishwater gray. Her T-shirt read PROPERTY OF ALCATRAZ, and her oversized slippers had been inherited, Lewis knew, from her dead husband, Fred.

"I do my best," she said, leading the way into the parlor, "but this place has seen better days . . ."

Of course, the Dearborns had been to Shornoway many times before, but always as visitors. It was a shock, Lewis realized, to come here to *live*, especially for someone as particular as his mother. Mrs. Dearborn limped slowly across the cracked linoleum, leaning

18

on the cane she needed for her knee problem. Glancing around at the wallpaper—pink tulips, stained with yellow-brown streaks—she let out a derisive snort. Her gaze fixed on Great-Granddad's favorite chair, an oversized monstrosity the color of crusted gravy. Stuffing sprouted like toadstools through a dozen holes. Slowly, her eyes closed.

"Perhaps a few flowers?" said Mrs. Binchy.

"Mrs. Binchy, thank you," said Lewis's father. "We'll . . . er, manage."

"I'll see what I can do about that oven then. It's on the fritz again."

Lewis followed her to the kitchen. "Mrs. Binchy? Great-Granddad left me something in his will. He—"

"The ship!" said Mrs. Binchy. "Yes, dear, I heard. You'll want the key to the tower room. Now where did it get to?"

She shifted a dripping jam pot on the counter. "Ah. Here!"

Lewis stared. The key was like a key in a fairy tale—long and thin with interesting, complicated bits at the end.

"Straight up the back staircase," said Mrs. Binchy. "You know where that is?"

Lewis nodded. "But isn't it closed off?" For as long as he could remember, a rough plywood wall, covered with pink insulation, had blocked the back stairs.

"Not anymore. I had a fellow come yesterday to bash it open. Up the stairs, turn right, all the way to the last door."

Lewis hesitated, wanting to ask more, but the housekeeper's head was already in the oven. Banging noises emerged.

The old staircase creaked as he climbed the steep, narrow steps. His nose tickled in the dry, fusty air, and he fought back a sneeze. Reaching the next floor, he tiptoed down a hall, where he passed several doors. One was open, exposing a rusty bed frame.

The end of the hall was dark. Lewis fumbled with the key, trying not to breathe the stale air. At last, the lock clicked. The door swung open into the tower.

A gust of fresh sea breeze hit him like a blow, ruffling his hair and ballooning his T-shirt away from his body. He stepped forward, surprised, and squinted in the bright sunlight. Eight high walls formed an octagon—almost a circle—around him. Three of them had the tall windows that faced the ocean. The middle window was open, its torn lace curtains tossing in the wind.

Lewis blinked and caught his breath. There was something unusual about this room. Something that made it completely different from the rest of

Shornoway. The wind, of course. The bright light. The blue-and-white wallpaper, with its cheery pattern of stripes and anchors.

But something else, too. Something welcoming. Maybe it was the roundness. No sharp edges or tight corners.

On one side was a short, narrow door, painted red. Lewis walked over and tried it, rattling the knob. Locked.

He moved on to a small brass bed, covered by an old striped mattress. It felt springy when he sat down. He bounced a few times, raising dust. Then he crossed to a chest-high cabinet, painted green, its glass doors crisscrossed with lead. Some of the glass was broken. Lewis peered inside.

Toys! Old ones. The kind you see in museums. He opened the doors, careful not to disturb the broken glass, and checked the top shelf. A striped wooden top. A wind-up bear holding a drum. Dusty tin soldiers. Lewis took three soldiers out and lined them up on top of the cabinet.

The next shelf held old books. Lewis pulled one out at random. *Little Lord Fauntleroy.*

And that's when he got it. This was a kid's room. At least, it had been once. He squatted to peer at the next shelf down. Three jars. One was filled with seashells, another with round white stones. A third held weathered pieces of colored glass.

Shells, stones, glass . . .

Suddenly, a memory came to him, as clear as if it were happening now. When Lewis was six or seven, he had walked down the cliff path to the ocean, Great-Granddad holding his hand. Treasure hunting, the old man called it. *Let's see what the sea has brought us, Sonny Boy.* Shells, colored glass, a dead starfish.

Such stories Lewis had heard on those walks! He got a shiver now, remembering. True stories, scary and dazzling. How Great-Granddad had joined the navy during the war. How he'd crossed the Atlantic in a hurricane. How his ship had been hit by a torpedo at night. How he'd been thrown into dark, icy water and come *this close* to drowning.

Lewis glanced at the book in his hand. Opening it to the title page, he read:

To Clement on his ninth birthday.
With dearest love from
Uncle Albert and Aunt Theodora

Clement? Great-Granddad's first name was Clement! This had been *his* room. Great-Granddad must have lived here when he was young.

Lewis looked back at the cabinet. One shelf left. The bottom one, thick with cobwebs. Squinting, he could see the outline of a fat bottle, lying on its side.

A wave of excitement surged through him. Gently, he reached in. He carried the bottle to the window, blew away the worst of the cobwebs and held it to the light.

Yes! Something inside. He rubbed the glass with his hand.

There it was, between the streaks. A model of an old-fashioned sailing ship. Three-masted, with tiny yellowing sails.

But the bottle was still dirty. Lewis glanced down at his white T-shirt. Quickly, before he could change his mind, he whipped it off and rubbed it fiercely against the bottle.

Peering inside again, he began to shiver—partly, of course, because of the cool breeze on his bare skin. But *some* goosebumps, there was no question, were coming from excitement at the sight of a tiny sailor, perched in a crow's nest at the top of the main mast, so small Lewis wouldn't have noticed him except for his startlingly red jacket. The sailor was holding up his right arm. He seemed to be *waving* at Lewis!

Footsteps sounded in the hall. Lewis scrambled to pull on his T-shirt.

"Ah, here you are. Your mother's been looking for you." Mr. Dearborn stepped inside. "Well, *this* room's in better shape than the rest. Not much used, I suppose. What've you got there?"

Lewis held up the bottle.

"Is that it? Granddad's ship?"

He joined Lewis at the window just as a gust of wind lifted the lace curtain. It draped itself over Mr. Dearborn's bald head like a bridal veil. Lewis hid a smile.

Mr. Dearborn brushed away the curtain, then caught his breath. "Gosh! Will you look at that?" Leaning both hands on the windowsill, he gazed at the Atlantic Ocean. "Quite a view, Lewis. I bet if you had binoculars, you could see Portugal out this window. Heh, heh. France and England. Maybe Africa, too."

Lewis knew this was silly, but he scanned the horizon all the same. Those places *were* out there. His chest swelled with sea air—and something he couldn't name—as he took in the enormous expanse of open sky, and beneath it, the waves rolling in from . . .

Everywhere!

In that moment, he knew what he wanted. Desperately.

"Dad?"

"Yes?"

"Can I have this room?"

It wasn't just the view. It was something much stronger, and more than a little strange. Lewis had never been in this room before. But he felt as if he *belonged* here, as he had never belonged anywhere in his life.

Mr. Dearborn cleared his throat. "Your mother's already picked a room for you, Lewis. Downstairs. I suppose you can ask, though."

Slow footsteps sounded in the hall, punctuated by cane clicks. A moment later, Mrs. Dearborn's frame—large and sturdy, firmly encased in a beige pantsuit—filled the doorway. It's no use, thought Lewis, she'll never agree. It was amazing she had climbed up here at all.

Lewis wondered, not for the first time, what it would be like to have *young* parents. The kind who wore jeans.

"Charlotte, look," said his father. "Lewis found his ship."

Lewis held it up.

His mother let out a sigh. "Lewis, it's filthy. *You're* filthy! Look at your hands. And what have you done to your shirt?" She beckoned him to come and began brushing at the smears.

"But . . ." Lewis looked at his father pleadingly.

If his father understood, he didn't speak.

Lewis screwed up his courage. "Mom? I was wondering . . . I'd like . . . I mean, I'd *really* like to have this room. For me. To be my bedroom."

Mrs. Dearborn frowned. "This room? But that's ridiculous. It's miles from anywhere."

"I don't mind." Lewis was shocked to hear himself arguing. He almost never argued with his mother. But here he was, continuing. "I *like* to be by myself. I'll clean it and fix it up. I like this room because it's so . . ." He thought quickly. "Round!"

Mr. Dearborn chuckled. "That's true, Charlotte. It *is* much rounder than the other rooms. Lots of space, too. Lewis could spread out here. Invite his friends home." He smiled cheerfully, having never noticed, apparently, that Lewis didn't invite friends home.

"Gerald, please," said Mrs. Dearborn. "What if he has one of his night terrors?"

"I haven't had nightmares for years," protested Lewis. Would she bring up the bed-wetting, too? He hadn't done *that* since he was five!

Mr. Dearborn cleared his throat. "Well, of course, it's up to you. But he *is* getting older, isn't he? Quite a young man, really, and—"

"He's *not* a man," said Lewis's mother firmly. "He's an eleven-year-old boy."

In the silence that followed, there was the soft *chuk* of something hitting the floor. All three Dearborns turned to look. A toy soldier had fallen off the cabinet.

Mrs. Dearborn sucked in her breath. "Oh!" she said. "Lewis, bring it to me, please."

He ran to obey.

She cradled the toy in her hands. "I *know* these soldiers. When I was little, and my parents brought me here to visit Granddad—Grandmother was alive then, too, of course—I sometimes played in this room. I'd forgotten." As she stared at the tiny figure, her gaze softened.

Lewis suddenly knew that this moment—now!— was his only chance. "Can I stay here, Mom? Please? It's the kid's room, right? For the kid in the family?"

She didn't speak.

Mr. Dearborn sniffed the air. "Smells fresh up here. You *did* say, Charlotte, that the downstairs bedroom smells of mold. Not good for Lewis's lungs, I suppose—mold."

Mrs. Dearborn blinked. The dreamy look was gone, replaced by worry. Lewis knew what she was thinking. Mold. His asthma! Of course, he didn't actually *have* asthma—the doctor had said so, flat out. But his mother continued to insist that he *did* have it, along with a lot of other things he didn't have. Anemia. Tonsillitis. Food allergies.

He waited, shifting from foot to foot, as she sniffed the fresh air. How lucky that the window had been open when he arrived!

"All right," she said finally. "We'll give it a try. Mind you, it's only temporary. We'll work something else out for winter."

Lewis nodded so hard, he felt dizzy. Was he really going to be allowed to *live* here?

His mother was dusting him off again. "Change your shirt, Lewis. Now. Before the moving men come."

Lewis had *seen* the moving men. They were sweaty and overweight, and their T-shirts were disgusting. But he nodded again, barely able to contain his glee.

As he followed his parents out, he looked around one last time. Then he reached for the doorknob.

And that's when he saw it. A series of letters, small and rough, carved into the middle section of the door, probably with a penknife. The kind of letters a boy might carve into his bedroom door, knowing they would get him into trouble. When Lewis saw what the letters spelled, he gasped.

LIBERTALIA

4

L ewis practically danced down the back stairs.

He couldn't believe it. The *room* was Libertalia! Great-Granddad had sent him to the tower room so that he would see it and love it and want it for his own. And that's what had happened. The *room* was Great-Granddad's real gift.

As for why he had called it Libertalia? Well, who could say? Maybe Great-Granddad had played pirate games there when he was little. Maybe it was like calling your room the Jolly Roger.

The first thing Lewis did was clean it. He began by sweeping the floor. Then, using hot soapy water, he scrubbed the doors, the windows and the dusty furniture. His dad had offered to clear the broken glass in the green cabinet, so he left that alone. But on *top* of the cabinet, he placed his ship in a bottle, now spotless and gleaming. It looked great beside the tin soldiers.

While he was cleaning, the moving men arrived, carrying his desk, bed and dresser. They tried to take the old brass bed away, but Lewis begged to keep it.

"I'll use it as a couch!" he said.

He unpacked his clothes and his other belongings. He set up his onyx chess set, a gift from his father, on top of the dresser. Mr. Dearborn loved chess and had been excited to teach Lewis the game, especially when it became clear that Lewis had a knack for it. Lewis wasn't good enough to beat his father yet, but he thought he might be getting close.

And finally, he traded his desk chair—orange plastic and too small for a sixth-grader—for a white wicker chair he found down the hall. It was old, of course, but he didn't mind that.

With the extra furniture, the tower was more crowded, but that only made it more appealing. There was nothing about this room that wasn't perfect! No old-house smells. No strangeness. Even though no one had lived there for years, it had a comfortable, lived-in feeling.

And even in the heat of noon, the air stayed fresh and cool. It was that middle window. No matter how often Lewis shut it, it popped open again. Not that he minded—he liked to stand in front of it and stare out and just breathe. The air through that window was the best he'd ever tasted.

That night, Lewis slept in Libertalia for the first time. The moon was almost full; it cast a pale glow through the tall windows. He could hear the ocean as clearly as if it were inside the room, and after a while, he noticed that he was breathing in rhythm with the crashing of the waves. In his dreams, he floated. Weightless.

He awoke at the first hint of orange-red sun, rising above the sea. The middle window was open. He ran straight to it. And what a fine burst of feeling he had then, with all the friendly clutter of Libertalia behind him and all the bright, open promise of the horizon in front.

This was *exactly* where he was supposed to be. Even the thought of school didn't scare him. Not if he had this room to come home to.

In the days that followed, he was happier than he'd ever been. His parents visited, but only twice. It was a long walk to Libertalia, especially for his mother, and they had a lot to do in the rest of the house. They were relieved, too, to discover that the strange-looking device above Libertalia's door was an old-fashioned intercom that linked to the kitchen. If they pressed a button in the kitchen, a bell would sound in the tower room.

"When you hear that bell," said his mother, "you come downstairs immediately. Do you understand me, Lewis?"

It was almost like being an orphan, he thought—the *good* kind, the kind in books, the kind who has adventures. And his parents hadn't even had to die! In his old house, his room had been right beside theirs. If he tried to read at night, they yelled, "Turn the light out, Lewis!" If he coughed, they hurried to his side with medicine. Both of them stomped in whenever they felt like it to check his homework or his temperature or his supply of clean socks. He might as well have lived in an airport!

But here? In Libertalia? It was like having his own apartment. He could run around naked!

Not that he'd want to.

He was so happy that when the noises began, he tried to ignore them. They came from behind the walls. Creaks. Thumps. Sometimes a low burble of voices. At first, the sounds were so quiet he could hardly hear them over the pounding of the waves. But as they got louder, he realized that they were coming from behind the narrow red door. After staring at it for most of an evening, it occurred to Lewis that the key Mrs. Binchy had given him might work in *that* door as well. He tried it and was delighted when the red door sprang open. But all he'd revealed was a small, empty closet. It smelled of fish.

Lewis didn't *want* to hear the noises. He wanted them to go away, and for the next few days, he did his best to block them out. But on his sixth day in the tower, after some particularly loud thumps, he went down to ask his father about it.

"It's nothing," said Mr. Dearborn. "Old houses are like that. Shifting and settling on their foundations. Especially with these winds."

Lewis nodded. "But . . . sometimes it sounds more like voices."

"Oh? Well, that would be me and your mother, I suppose. Our voices traveling through the pipes. We'll have to watch what we say, won't we? No more secrets from Lewis! Heh, heh."

Mr. Dearborn's jokes were almost always bad. But Lewis laughed at this one, out of relief. He returned to Libertalia feeling better.

The window was open. Again! He was about to close it when he heard a *thok* behind him. He turned. One of the toy soldiers had fallen onto the floor. He went to pick it up. Before he could, the second soldier fell. Then the third.

The wind? It didn't seem strong enough. He shut the window.

That's when he heard the *ping*. Jerking around, he saw that a nickel—part of a handful of change he had dumped on his desk—had fallen to the wooden floor. As he watched, the rest of the change, one coin after another, slid off the desk. *Ping, ping, ping . . . ping.*

Holding his breath, Lewis walked to the desk. He slid his hand along its surface. It was slanted. It *must* be.

Or maybe the floor was slanted?

As he bent to retrieve the coins, he realized, with a hammering of his heart, that he was wrong. The floor wasn't slanted. *Nothing* was slanted. Because, as he watched, one of the quarters on the floor rose slowly into the air. It hovered above the desk briefly before dropping slowly onto its surface. Then, as Lewis struggled to believe his eyes, a dime rose from the floor.

He let out a scream. At least, he *tried* to, but all that came out was the kind of thin, helpless squeak people make in nightmares.

He ran for the door and yanked the knob. The door wouldn't budge. Frantic, he kicked it, still trying to scream. But even the weak sounds he managed were muffled by something cool pressed against his mouth and upper body as he was pinned, with a thud, against the wall.

There was a swirling like mist all around, and a deep voice said in his ear, "Awrrr, laddie, there's no need to be afeared."

5

Lewis froze, rigid with fear. Only his eyes moved, flickering like a wild animal's.

There was no one there!

Cold air enveloped him, tinged with a whiff of fish. He exploded, without thinking, into terrified struggle, flailing his limbs. All in vain. He was pinned to the wall as securely as a fly beneath a swatter.

"Now, laddie, I just needs a wee moment, that's all. I'm . . . well, let's say I'm a friend of your great-granddaddy."

Chest heaving, Lewis sucked in great mouthfuls of air. Where was the voice coming from? He lashed out again.

"He were a fine man," said the voice, "and we was fond of one another, being two old sea dogs. Even if we quarreled now and then, it were a friendly sort of thing. He told me you'd be coming."

The mist swirled again. The voice *seemed* to be coming from its movement.

"Me?" whispered Lewis.

"Aye, you. He said you were a bold 'un."

"*Me?*" said Lewis again.

"Aye, but as I watches you, I has me doubts."

The hair on the back of Lewis's neck stood up. "You've been . . . watching me?"

"Aye, lad, and if there's any of your great-granddad's boldness in you, it's well hidden. And that's a worry to me, see. Because we needs someone with a sharp eye and a strong hand."

Lewis's heart was pounding so hard, he felt it would burst through his chest. There was a long moment when his mouth moved and no sound came out.

"Who *are* you?" he finally managed.

A rough laugh came back. "That's it, lad. Ask away! I'm James Crawley, at your service—Captain James Crawley, although it be more than two hunnert years since I've walked the decks of me own ship. Still, lad, you're here to fix that, ain't you?"

Lewis was suddenly even more terrified. "I . . . I don't know what you're talking about," he said. "I can't fix anything. I don't know you. I can't even *see* you!"

"Ah, you wants to *see* Captain Crawley, does you?" said the voice. "Better be sure, lad. There were a time when I were as sweet-looking as you. But I've lost me best bits over the years, and I ain't so pretty now. Are you brave enough to look on Captain Crawley as he be?"

Lewis didn't feel brave at all. His whole body was shaking, his hands worst of all, so he clenched them in an effort to keep them still. But he couldn't help thinking that, however awful it might be to see Captain Crawley, it couldn't be worse than *not* seeing him and not knowing who—or what—he was talking to.

Lewis's voice was uncertain as he replied, "Yes?"

He watched as the mist formed a grayish cloud. It circled like a tiny tornado and then slowly settled into the outline of a human body—transparent at first, then gradually becoming more solid.

"Aaaahhh," said Captain Crawley. He was facing away, toward the sea. From behind, Lewis could see a mane of tangled hair that might have been brown once, but was now grizzled and gray. It looked like old rope that had come unstrung.

The captain shook out his shoulders, rolled his neck and strutted to the window. Lewis took this chance to try again to break away from the wall. But something—what?—still held him there.

"There ain't nothing in this world like a good salt breeze," said the captain. He wore boots of worn black leather and a mottled, reddish jacket that hung almost to his knees.

Suddenly, he turned, revealing a face that would have made Lewis leap backward if he weren't already plastered against the wall. It was pockmarked all over, with a lumpy nose, and a smile that revealed several missing teeth. But it was his eyes that caught Lewis's attention. The right one, brown, glared at him fiercely. The left was nothing but a slit, showing white between half-closed lids.

Lewis forced himself to lower his gaze, bringing it to rest on the soft leather sash around the captain's waist. Tucked into it were a cutlass, a knife and an old-fashioned pistol. And there, clutched in the captain's right hand, was the last piece of the puzzle—a faded black three-cornered hat.

The hat was a dead giveaway.

"You're . . ." he tried, and then again, "you're . . . a pirate."

"A pirate? Well, lad, that ain't a word I likes. You may call me"—he bowed low, sweeping the ground with one hand—"a gentleman of fortune."

Narrowing his right eye, he gave Lewis a searching glance. "And besides, a man cannot be a pirate without he has a ship. That's why your great-granddad sent *you*."

Lewis's head was throbbing. "I—what do you mean, sent me?"

"Well, roughly speaking, it's this." Captain Crawley stroked his chin. "We needs you, young Lewis. Me and the boys."

"The boys?" squeaked Lewis. "You mean, there are . . . more of you?"

"Oh, aye," said Crawley, and he yelled back over his shoulder. "Come on out, mates!"

In front of the red door, a new cloud swirled and shimmered. As Lewis watched, it formed itself into a thin, ragged, hunched-over sailor with a long nose and a wide, wet mouth.

"Jack the Rat," said Captain Crawley. "Make your bow to the lad, Jack. Nice and polite now."

Jack didn't bow so much as bend his knobby knees, visible through the rips in his pants. The knees, like the rest of him, were filthy. Narrowing his eyes, he peered at Lewis with a look that a spider might give a fly.

Lewis flinched, but his attention was drawn immediately to a third misty figure. It took shape as a round-bellied man with pink cheeks and a greasy white beard. He looked almost like Santa, if you could ignore the jagged scar that sliced down his forehead and divided his right eyebrow in two.

"Is that 'im?" said the man.

"Aye," said Crawley.

"A bit small, ain't he?"

"Shut your trap, Moyle," said Jack the Rat. "He's big enough for what *we* wants." He grinned wetly at Lewis, licking his lips in such a terrifying way that Lewis was convinced the apparition meant to *eat* him.

Lewis struggled again. But when a fourth pirate appeared, an arm's length away, he was shocked into stillness. This pirate was *precisely* at arm's length, and the way Lewis knew that was because this pirate—a terrifyingly large man—was the one who was pinning him to the wall. He's a giant, thought Lewis. He's out of a fairy tale! Easily eight feet tall, the pirate had black hair, a thick black beard and coarse black hair covering what could be seen of his body. His hands, big as roasting pans, rested on Lewis's shoulders.

"You puts up a good fight," rumbled the giant. "I had to use two hands to hold you."

"See?" said Jack the Rat to no one in particular. "The lad's big enough."

"Big enough for what?" squeaked Lewis. Normally,

he was shy with strangers. But when a person is shocked to the bone, as Lewis was, and wondering if he's about to be eaten, shyness is apt to get pushed aside.

"Now don't be afeared," said Captain Crawley softly. "Barnaby Bellows is like a big puppy, ain't you, Bellows?"

The giant leered into Lewis's face. "I likes the lad's red hair," he said, his breath reeking of dead fish. "Red hair shows spirit!"

And that was just the beginning. Three more pirates followed. There was Skittles, tiny, bald and missing an arm. Jonas came next, lean, brown-skinned and shivering. He, too, had missing parts—two fingers on his left hand.

Last of all, and slowest to manifest himself, was Adam.

"Why, look at these two," said Moyle, glancing back and forth between Adam and Lewis. "They're the same age, ain't they? Two young lads as could be born the same day."

"Excepting," said Jack the Rat, "that young Adam here was born in 1786, if I recalls right."

"You recalls right," said Adam, staring at Lewis.

The boys *did* appear to be the same age. Adam was shorter, and his long fair hair was tied back in a pigtail. But Lewis could recognize a sixth-grader when he saw one.

Except, he remembered, that Adam was . . .

A ghost?

He still couldn't believe it. But what other explanation could there be?

"Adam's our ship's boy," said Crawley, "and though he be young, he's as stalwart in battle as any."

Adam, meanwhile, was studying Lewis's face. "Did you have the pox?" he asked finally.

Lewis blinked back, confused.

"Naaaahh!" said Crawley. "Those marks ain't pox scars. Them are just *freckles*! The lad's got freckles like a dog's got fleas."

This got a huge laugh from the pirates, all except Adam, who was staring now at Lewis's green T-shirt and khaki shorts. When he got to Lewis's shoes, his eyes widened. "Oooooh," he said. "Boots for a prince."

Lewis looked down. "They're just . . . running shoes."

"Running," repeated Adam. He knelt for a closer look. "Aye, a boy could run far in such boots."

At that, all the pirates became transfixed by Lewis's shoes. Even Barnaby Bellows glanced down, relaxing his grip on Lewis's shoulders.

It was like a signal.

Lewis bolted!

44

But when he reached the door, Crawley was there, blocking his way. "Not so fast, laddie. We won't hold you long, I promise, but we needs you to hear us out."

"Aye," chorused the others. "Hear us out!"

Lewis tried to stop his knees from quivering. "Just tell me what you want," he begged.

Crawley smiled his gap-toothed smile. "We wants you to help us get our ship back."

It was like a horrible riddle.

"I don't understand," said Lewis.

Crawley pointed at the bottle on Lewis's shelf.

"You want me to . . . get your ship out of that bottle?"

The pirates shouted with laughter, slapping their thighs.

"Nay," said Crawley with a final guffaw. "That's just a model, boy. Our ship—our *Maria Louisa*—she's sitting in a little house, down by the bay. Your great-granddad told us so. Four years ago, they brought her from some other place—"

"Halifax, it were," said Moyle.

"Aye," said Crawley. "And a miracle, by thunder, to hear of her after so many years. They took her to that little house—"

"It were called a moo-see-um," said Moyle, nodding wisely. "That's what the granddaddy said."

45

Lewis blinked in comprehension. "You mean the Maritime Museum?" The Tandy Bay Maritime Museum was one of the town hall buildings, right beside the ocean, at the center of town. "They *did* bring a ship there. I saw it on a school trip."

"Aye," said Jonas, in a voice filled with pride. "And that ship? She's ours!"

Barnaby Bellows thumped his huge fist on the desk. "Ours!" he yelled.

"She *was* ours," said Crawley, his voice rising with anger, "until she were stolen from us, in dead of night. Attacked, we was, by that son of a dogfish, John Edward Dire! He *could* have put us ashore. It were only fair and right. But, oh, laddie . . . he were the devil's spawn, that Captain Dire, and so were his crew. They laughed as they kilt us. Laughed!"

"K-killed you?" repeated Lewis.

"Aye," growled Crawley. "Tied us up, hand and foot, all together with the one rope. Hurled us overboard. We was helpless as babes."

"Sank like stones!" muttered Moyle.

"Dropped to the bottom with nary a bubble," added Skittles.

"But at least," said Adam, "we washed up here together."

"Aye," agreed Jonas, "we did. Except for Laughing Harry."

At that, the pirates went glum and silent.

Lewis was almost afraid to ask. "Who's Laughing Harry?"

"Our navigator," said Crawley. "And a finer man never lived! Until he were keelhauled by Dire."

"Keelhauled?"

"Aye," muttered Crawley. "Keelhauled, laddie, is when they ties you to a rope and drags you under the ship's bottom from one end to t'other. Does you know what's on the bottom of a ship? Barnacles sharp as razors, that's what. Shells as will rip your skin off—if you survive the haul, that is. Most men don't. Poor Harry! He vanished forever under the *Maria Louisa*. Never even come up."

"Only the rope," sighed Skittles, "all ragged and torn."

"Sharks!" said Jack the Rat. "They smells blood, even through the water."

"A nasty end," said Moyle. "Can't even be a ghost! Not after the sharks gets you."

"He weren't laughing *that* day," added Jonas. "Poor, poor Harry."

The pirates lapsed into reverent silence. But for Lewis, the story hadn't ended.

"And then . . . then you moved in here?"

"Nah," said Moyle. "This house weren't built yet. We lived in a cave, them first years. It were down the beach, half mile north."

"You haunted a cave?" said Lewis to himself. At least, he *thought* he said it to himself.

"We don't calls it haunting." Crawley gave Lewis an irritated glance. "Me and the boys, we don't go around clanking chains or moaning or all that bilgewater. We just . . . what you would call, makes ourselves to *home*."

"It were *terrible* nasty and cold in that cave," said Jonas, shivering fiercely at the memory. "Especially in winter! And we was there for many a year. So when this big house were built, this Shornoway, we was glad to come inside and make ourselves a nice, cozy place here."

Watching Jonas shiver, Lewis couldn't help wondering if he had *ever* gotten over the effects of the cave.

"Aye," said Crawley, as if he were reading Lewis's mind, "that cave were a misery, especially for our Jonas, being used to a warmer clime. And all these years since—"

"Centuries!" said Moyle.

"All these *centuries*," repeated Crawley, "we's been glad to have a home here with your family. Part of the family ourselves, you might say. Still, we knows where our *real* home is—on our ship. The *Maria Louisa*! Ever since we heard from your great-granddad that our ship were found and stowed in that little moo-see-um, why, we've been aiming to get ourselves there."

"It's where we belongs," said Moyle. "Your granddaddy, he promised to take us to that moo-see-um himself. But he were just too old! Couldn't do it."

"We's been waiting for *you*, lad," said Skittles softly. "You'll help us, won't you?"

The pirates all turned plaintive eyes on Lewis.

"Me?" He shrank back. "Why do you need *my* help? Why can't you just go there if you want?"

The pirates looked suddenly uncomfortable.

"Well, me and the boys," said Captain Crawley, glancing around at his crew, most of whom were staring at the floor, "we been here a long time."

"We doesn't get out much," mumbled Skittles.

"That's not true," said Moyle, giving Skittles a cuff. "We went to that picnic, didn't we?"

"You mean the church picnic?" said Skittles. "The one where we scared that poor skinny preacher fellow off the bridge? Why, that were back in 1902."

"Were it really?" said Moyle in amazement. "That long ago?"

"Aye, it were a fine day in—"

"Stow it!" roared Crawley. He turned to Lewis with a sickly-sweet smile. "You see, lad, we needs your help because some of us have, well . . . settled in. Gone soft, like."

Lewis tried to understand. "Are you saying you're . . . scared?"

The gasp that followed came from every pirate in the room.

"Scared?" snarled Jack the Rat. "I'll show you how scared we be." Hauling out his cutlass, he lunged toward Lewis. Barnaby Bellows had to hold him back.

"Of course we ain't scared." Captain Crawley stepped neatly between them. "We're blackguards! Scoundrels! Lived rough as nails and died a rougher death. We're afeared of nothing!"

"Excepting maybe . . ." said Skittles, watching the captain warily, "them things that move so fast."

Murmurs of agreement followed, even in the face of Crawley's glowering.

"What things?" asked Lewis.

"On the roads," breathed Skittles hoarsely. "We seen 'em. They go like lightning."

"Try to get across a road," added Bellows, "and them things runs right through you!"

"You mean . . ." Lewis struggled to understand. "Cars?"

"Cars! Aye, that's what they're called." Skittles shuddered. "It's unnatural how fast they go."

"But . . ." said Lewis, then petered out. He didn't know where to begin explaining things like traffic rules and pedestrian crossings to a crew of pirate ghosts.

"We tried going to that moo-see-um," said Jonas. "But them car-things! They got us every time."

"That's why we wants *you* to take us there," said Crawley. "Past them things and into that little house where the *Maria Louisa* be waiting."

Lewis chewed his lip, unsure of what they knew. "There's a police station there. It's right beside the museum."

"Police?" snarled Jack. "The law?" He whipped out a dagger and brandished it in the air. "*We'll* give 'em a taste, we will! We'll slice out their gizzards!"

"Slice 'em out!" chorused Jonas and Bellows.

Crawley hissed sharply, his hand raised in a warning gesture. Then, offering Lewis another wheedling smile, he spoke in the kind of soft, gentle voice you might use for a baby. "All we wants, laddie, is for you to give it some thought."

Backing away from Lewis then, and also from the door, Crawley settled himself on the wicker chair. "Just a wee ponder," he said. "Ain't that right, boys?"

Taking their cues, the others found places around the room. Skittles and Moyle each sank onto a bed, while Bellows, Adam and Jonas settled on the floor. Jack the Rat swept Lewis's chess set to the floor with a clatter, before hoisting his filthy body onto the dresser.

Lewis hardly dared breathe. Were they really going to let him go? The door, just steps away, was like a dream.

He got there in two leaps.

As he struggled with the knob, fingers slippery with fear, he waited for hands to grab him. He could almost *feel* the cold, ghostly fingers on his shoulders.

The knob turned.

He yanked the door open and ran.

7

Skidding down the hall—stumbling, scrambling up—he expected any second to hear a shouted "Laddie!" from behind. But the only sound was his own feet, pounding the floor.

He hit the stairs in an explosion of thuds and didn't stop till he reached his father's study, a small room at the end of a hall. Gasping, he reached for the doorknob . . .

And stopped.

He stared at his shaking hand. Wait, he told himself. Think!

What would happen if he told his father?

His father would tell his mother, of course. Then what?

It was *possible* they'd believe him. But the more he thought about it, the less likely this seemed. All his life, they'd taught him that ghosts—or monsters or aliens, any such things—were "nonsense." Even Santa and the Easter Bunny had been half-hearted visitors to the Dearborn house.

And if they didn't believe him, what then? Would they think he was nuts? Lying? Having nightmares in broad daylight? What would they do?

Worry, that's what. They worried about *everything*, his parents—in different ways, true, but they would get together on this. He didn't have to think long to realize that a story about pirate ghosts would turn into a worry so huge—so absolutely *colossal*, in fact—he wouldn't get a moment alone for the next year! They'd send him to that child psychologist again, the one who'd tried to get him to play with stuffed animals.

The study door opened.

"Ah, Lewis, it's you." His father frowned. "You're panting. Are you all right?"

"Fine. Just . . . running."

"Would you like to come in?"

Lewis ducked inside and dropped into a chair. He didn't have to *say* anything. He could just sit.

"Are you sure nothing's wrong?" Mr. Dearborn peered over his glasses.

Lewis glanced around. There was a parcel on his father's desk. One side was open, revealing a thick stack of paper.

"Is that your book?"

Mr. Dearborn ran his fingers through the last few hairs on his balding scalp. He tried to smile. "It's come back. Again. That's eleven now."

Lewis struggled to focus. Eleven. That meant publishers. The parcel contained the book his father had written, *Daily Life Among the Ancient Minoans*. As Mr. Dearborn often said, the book had been *his* daily life for more than six years. It was 693 pages long, and Lewis was sure it must tell everything that was ever known about the ancient Minoans and therefore be a book many people would want to read. But the publishers kept turning it down.

"Don't worry," said Lewis automatically. "Someone will publish it. Next time."

Mr. Dearborn shook his head. "This was my last chance. There aren't any other publishers who do this sort of book."

"Oh!" Lewis was shocked into genuine attention. He had never imagined his father could run out of publishers.

"Ah, well." Mr. Dearborn sat down and stared at a

blank spot on the wall. Clasping his fingers together, he pressed them against his lips.

Lewis watched, his panic giving way to sadness. "You could get another teaching job. In a college. Right?"

"What?" said his father in a flat monotone. "Oh, sure. Maybe."

But Lewis knew this wouldn't happen. He wasn't sure why his father had lost his teaching job and couldn't get another one. But he suspected, from bits he'd overheard, that his father wasn't a good enough teacher. His mother, who also taught at a college—mathematics, not Minoans—had tried to coach his father to become better at teaching. In the end, though, Mr. Dearborn had given up. He'd written his book instead.

Lewis took a deep breath. His heart wasn't beating *quite* so hard now. He held out his right hand. Almost still.

"I think I'll sleep down here tonight," he said and waited for his father to ask why.

But his father just kept staring at the wall through smudged glasses. "Oh? Well, sure. That's fine."

Lewis left. He wandered into the parlor and settled into a rocking chair. Rocking jerkily, desperate to understand, he began to re-live his morning—every terrifying moment.

Was it true that Great-Granddad had sent him to the

pirates? If so, the old man really *had* lost his marbles. Even he should have seen that Lewis was not the kind of boy who could lead a gang of pirate ghosts through the town of Tandy Bay—and past the Tandy Bay police station! He was the last boy on *earth* who could do such a thing. Great-Granddad should have known that.

The more he thought about it, the more he saw it as an awful trick. It was like sending him into a cage full of tigers. Lewis could hardly believe his own relative would do such a thing.

He thought back, remembering how Great-Granddad used to shout at the furniture. It hadn't been the *furniture*. Lewis could see that now. Great-Granddad had been yelling at the pirates. He knew them well! And before he died, he had set Lewis up. His own great-grandson.

Libertalia. You!

That night, Lewis slept on a pullout couch in the tiny room beside his parents. The corners were crammed with boxes, and the air had a sour smell that made him breathe through his mouth. A single small window faced the driveway, with a view of the family car. Instead of crashing waves, he heard his mother's voice, complaining through the wall.

"The water pressure's non-existent. Half an hour to run a bath. It *trickles* out."

His father mumbled a reply.

"Nothing works! The furnace is an antique."

Another mumble. Longer.

"Well, *I* know why he's sleeping downstairs. He's too young to be on his own. I told you that, didn't I?"

Lewis rammed his head into his pillow. But his parents' voices continued . . . mumble . . . electricity . . . mumble . . . toilets.

Shutting his eyes, he thought about Libertalia. He conjured up the blue-and-white walls, the ship in a bottle, the roaring sea. He imagined it so well that waking next morning, he thought he was there. What a shock to open his eyes and see his mother's old sewing machine and the bins labeled "Winter Clothes."

In the days that followed, his life became, like his new room, shrunken and drab. He tiptoed around the ground floor, trying to stay clear of the adults, alert for thuds or voices in the walls. He wanted to go down to the beach—he loved that beach!—but his mother wouldn't hear of it.

"It's not a swimming beach, Lewis. Those waves could pull you to your death."

"I know that," said Lewis. "I won't go in the water. I just want to look for shells and things."

"What if there's a rogue wave?" said his mother. "You're not to go down there without your father."

And what, Lewis wanted to ask, would his *father* do if a rogue wave leaped out of the ocean and swept them both away?

In any case, his father wasn't interested. Mr. Dearborn was taking this latest rejection of his book hard, spending long hours alone in his office. When he came out, he wandered like a sleepwalker. Mrs. Dearborn, meanwhile, seemed to have gained all the energy her husband had lost. She thumped through the house, giving orders to workmen—plumbers, telephone installers, appliance repairmen.

"I don't care if it's just six months," she told her husband. "It has to be liveable."

When she wasn't ordering workmen around, she was bossing Lewis. She only had to see him to find new chores.

"Break down these boxes, please, Lewis, and stack them in the shed. When you finish, you can get at those weeds in the driveway."

At night in his new downstairs room, there were tooth-flossing reminders and vitamin suggestions and shouted commands through the wall. "Lights out now. Go to sleep!"

And of course his mother was bound to notice that he'd been wearing the same clothes for days. "For heaven's sake, Lewis, how do you expect us to treat you like an adult? Put on a clean shirt!"

He headed obediently for the rear staircase. Halfway up, he lost his nerve. On the pretext of a broken lamp, he asked Mr. Dearborn to come with him.

So it was his father who opened the door to the tower this time. Lewis sniffed the air as he entered, but he hardly noticed the faint whiff of fish because Libertalia was already tugging at his heart . . . magical, exciting, unbearably familiar. Above all, welcoming. As if it had been waiting.

"Did you leave this window open again?" His father sounded irritated. "You *must* remember to shut it, Lewis. If it rains, the floor will get soaked."

I *did* shut it, thought Lewis. I could shut it a thousand times, it wouldn't do any good.

"And is this any way to treat your chess set?"

Lewis looked down. The chess pieces were still scattered across the floor, where Jack the Rat had flung them. Quickly, Lewis gathered them up, glad to see that none were broken.

He didn't look out at the ocean. It made him too sad.

"Is this the broken lamp?" His father was fiddling beside Lewis's bed. "Seems to work fine."

Lewis began stuffing clothes into a laundry bag. "I guess you fixed it. Thanks, Dad."

He didn't look back as they left. Stumbling down

the stairs, he felt as if—like the pirates—he'd lost an important body part. An arm, maybe. A leg.

The only bright spot in his life was food. After some discussion, Mrs. Binchy had been hired for the duration of the Dearborns' stay in Shornoway, mostly, Lewis figured, because she knew how to work the stove. His father's cooking skills were limited to toast, and his mother flatly refused to go near the stove—an enormous black monster so old it had once burned logs. Mrs. Dearborn avoided the entire kitchen, in fact, saying it would drive her crazy. Under Mrs. Binchy's rule, it was a spectacular mess—crusty pots in the sink, greasy puddles and vegetable peelings dotting the counters. But out of the chaos came the most incredible food. Freshly baked bread so meltingly light, it didn't need butter. Thick roast beefs that practically carved themselves. Hot apple tarts, cinnamon twists.

Lewis wasn't used to this. Food in his old house had been plain and sensible. Steamed vegetables. Baked fish. Boiled potatoes.

He *liked* the new food. He liked Mrs. Binchy, too, but he didn't like it when she asked questions.

"Not very interesting for you, is it, Lewis? Stuck here with us old fogies. Well, I suppose the only *real* fogy is me. Still, you'll be glad to get back to school and see your friends, won't you?"

Lewis nodded as if he was glad. But the blueberry muffin in his mouth, so delicious a moment before, had turned to sawdust.

And, suddenly, there was no more avoiding it.

School.

The night before, his mother set out his school clothes—the striped shirt and gray pants they had bought for the funeral. Lewis looked at them and knew at once they were wrong. But he wasn't sure why, and he couldn't begin to explain.

He stared at his ceiling till nearly 2 a.m. He thought about the pirates, who had stolen the only thing in his life that was any good. He thought about his great-granddad, who had tricked and betrayed him. And he thought about the next morning at school.

It was terrible. All of it.

But school was the worst.

8

The first day was a disaster.

He didn't expect it to go well, of course. But somehow, year after year, he was never prepared for how bad it could be.

First, there were his parents. They always came with him the first day, he knew that. But he always let himself hope that this year might be different.

"The other parents don't come," he said at breakfast.

"We're not other parents," said his mother.

It was hard to argue with that.

Of course, there were plenty of parents who drove their kids to Tandy Bay Elementary on the first day.

But they didn't come into the classrooms. Not if their kids were in sixth grade!

But there were Mr. and Mrs. Dearborn, large and bulky, wearing dark suits, pushing their way through the milling students to get to the teacher's desk. They looked like a couple of beetles on an ant hill.

"Excuse us," demanded his mother, holding out her cane to clear a path. "Pardon!"

Kids backed away, giggling.

The teacher stood up, surprised. She was new, Lewis saw—a pretty young woman with stylish blue glasses and blond hair tied back. She held out her hand. "I'm Ms. Forsley. Can I—"

"Charlotte Dearborn," said Lewis's mother firmly in a voice that carried into the hall. "*Dr.* Charlotte Dearborn. And this is my husband, Dr. Gerald Dearborn. We'd like a word about our son, Lewis."

The class grew quiet, the buzz of voices fading.

"Well—" said Ms. Forsley. But it was too late.

"Lewis is gifted, you understand, and he'll need special . . ."

Lewis forced his brain to sing la-la-la so he wouldn't have to listen. But he heard the laughter behind him and a boy's voice repeating "*Special!*" He heard Ms. Forsley's voice, too, pleasant and friendly, suggesting that they could discuss it later. The teachers *always* said this, every year, but his parents never learned.

La-la-la, went Lewis in his head, trying to block out "Lewis's health" and "fragile," and then "asthma" and "allergies." The other kids were beginning to sit down, so he shuffled sideways and dropped into an empty desk, wishing he could shrivel up like a raisin and fall through a crack in the floor. La-la-la, he continued—forever, it felt like—until Mrs. Dearborn *finally* stopped. Thunk, thunk went her cane down the aisle.

As she passed Lewis's desk, she paused.

What now, he thought. Suddenly, her hand came out, and—was she *really* smoothing down the hair at the back of his head? Was his cowlick sticking up again? Who on the whole, stupid planet *cared* if Lewis's hair stuck up?

His mother, that's who. She made a loud "tsk" sound.

Mr. Dearborn added his own good-bye—a fond pat on Lewis's shoulder. Finally, they were gone. Lewis let out all the breath he'd been holding in.

Then he waited, scrunched tight against the plastic of his chair. Sooner or later, Ms. Forsley would do it. Speak directly to him.

It didn't happen right away. When she took attendance, he managed to squeak out a "Here!" It sounded weird and got a few laughs, but she moved on quickly.

"Danny Divers?"

No answer. Lewis looked around.

"Does anybody know where Danny is?"

From the back, someone said, "He moved away at the beginning of summer."

Lewis felt a stab of disappointment. Danny Divers wasn't exactly his friend. More like an ally. He and Danny had been somehow on the same side. And now Danny was gone.

When attendance ended, Ms. Forsley welcomed the class and said all the usual things about having a good year together. Then she suggested that they begin by each telling one interesting thing they had done over the summer.

"I'll start," she said. "This summer I traveled to the Rocky Mountains with some friends to go hiking."

There was more, but Lewis didn't hear because of the roar in his ears. His heart began to pound, and his head and upper body filled with warmth. He heard the other kids saying . . . something. He tried to think of what *he* had done this summer. Moved to Shornoway, of course. But it didn't matter. It was hopeless. *He* was hopeless.

Some of the kids had long stories, so it took a while to get to him.

"And you, Lewis?" said Ms. Forsley.

The room went quiet.

She waited. The whole class waited.

Lewis felt heat, like flames from a furnace, rise through his body and flow into his face. He felt panic seize his muscles, holding them tight and rigid. He opened his mouth. Ms. Forsley leaned forward.

Nothing came out. Not even a grunt.

The silence grew.

"Lewis?" said Ms. Forsley.

The silence dragged on. Lewis knew what he looked like. Scarlet. His face was now the same reddish color as his hair. No. Brighter! Kids had *told* him how he looked when this happened. Like a human tomato.

At least he wasn't crying. Sometimes when this happened, tears ran down his face.

At least he wasn't doing that.

Finally, a voice spoke up. Seth Tyler's voice, polite. "He can't talk."

"What do you mean?" said Ms. Forsley. "Of course he can. Lewis?"

"No," insisted Seth, his voice not quite so polite anymore. "He can't talk in class. He never does. We'll sit here all *day* if you wait for him."

Muffled giggles followed.

"That's enough." Ms. Forsley sounded rattled. "Lewis, we'll give you another chance later. Now . . . um, Catherine?"

Another chance later. That was bad. It meant she would keep trying. Most of his teachers *did* keep trying. They thought it was their job to get Lewis to talk in class. They even gave grades for it. They called it participation. Or worse, oral presentation.

Lewis had seen a movie on TV once where the main character described himself as "terminally shy." The phrase stuck in Lewis's mind because that was exactly what *he* was. If it were possible to actually die of shyness, Lewis would have been in his grave long ago. Back in first grade, probably. That was the first time he had found himself in a class with other kids, his parents having kept him out of kindergarten because of a flu scare. Before first grade, it was just him and his parents and his nanny, Judith, who had looked after him when he was little. Judith was nice, but, like his parents, quite old, and looking back, Lewis figured that she must have been shy herself. At any rate, she never spoke to the other adults in the playground, so Lewis didn't talk to the kids, either. Not until first grade.

By then, it was too late. He knew nothing. He got everything wrong. Clothes, of course. He wore a *coat* that first year—a long blue coat that came down past his knees.

You couldn't play games in a coat! So tag and dodge

ball were among the things he got wrong. Some of the other things were lunch foods, recess, birthday presents, names of cars, taking turns, TV shows, sharing, Halloween costumes and talking.

Talking was the worst. He'd gotten that wrong immediately. He had talked way too much, he could see that now, and he didn't talk the way other kids did or about the same things. So they had stopped talking to him. They had stopped listening. They had stopped even seeing that he was there. He couldn't blame them, really.

But Lewis wasn't stupid, and he understood—even at six—that the other kids didn't like him, even if he didn't know why. So, little by little, he had given up. Eventually, he had ended up like that guy in the TV movie—terminally shy. He couldn't speak anymore in class. Not at *all*! In the past few years, he had said so little that his school voice had rusted right over. If he forced himself, what came out was the caw of a crow, or—like this morning—a rodent squeak.

When the recess bell rang, Lewis followed his classmates outside. He found a place to stand, beside the front stairs. Over the years, he'd developed a talent for finding corners of the schoolyard to hide in, walls to lean against. He was good at stillness, too—so good, kids ran past without seeing him, as if he were a stump. If Danny Divers were there, they might stand beside each other. Two stumps. They might say a few words now and then.

But Danny Divers was gone.

Lewis kept his head down, as if he had a powerful interest in his own shoes. A picture of an ostrich popped into his head—he'd heard that ostriches hide their heads in the sand, believing this makes them invisible. He smiled to think that he was really no smarter than an ostrich.

"What's so funny, Lewisssssser?" said a voice to his right.

Seth.

Lewis didn't answer.

"I guess he won't talk to us," said Seth. "Maybe it's because he's so *special*."

Lewis stared at the shoes in the semi-circle around him. He knew Seth's shoes well. White trainers, heavily scuffed, with a couple of blue stripes. White pants. Lewis knew without looking up that the T-shirt was white, too. This had been Seth's uniform ever since he'd turned up after Christmas the previous year. White shirt, white pants, every day. Nobody had ever dressed that way at Tandy Bay Elementary before. But Seth was the opposite of Lewis. He made friends easily. Soon there were two more boys dressing in white. And by June, two more.

Now, glancing around, Lewis could see, above the shoes, six pairs of white pants. Maybe they were on sale, he thought, and his mouth once again betrayed him with a smile.

"Must be hilarious, Lewissssser," said Seth. "You're a regular comedian."

The other boys laughed.

"But guess what's *not* funny. You're standing in my square again."

Yes, thought Lewis, this was how it started.

The front of the schoolyard was covered in paving stones, each about the size of a desk top. It didn't matter which square Lewis stood on—that was the one Seth would want. It didn't help, either, to leave the paving-stone area. Seth would draw a square around Lewis in the dirt if he had to. Just so he could claim it.

"I don't suppose you'd mind *moving*, Lewissssser. I mean, I know you're *fragile* and all, but even us ordinary guys who aren't so *special* need a place to hang out. Know what I mean?" Guffaws from the other boys. The blue-and-white shoes took a step closer.

"Move!" ordered Seth.

Spotting a gap in the circle, Lewis darted through. He headed for the swings where Mrs. Reber, the playground supervisor, had joined hands with a circle of little girls. If he got close enough to her, Seth might leave him alone. If he got *too* close, Seth would notice and come after him later, calling him a baby. There was a perfect distance—close, but not too close—if only he could figure it out. Last year, he'd spent a lot of time trying.

This year it would be worse. Six guys already in Seth's white gang. And it was only the first day.

In the afternoon, Ms. Forsley tried him again with a question. An easier question—or so she thought. They were discussing what the class would do during gym time.

"How about you, Lewis? Do you like sports?"

Yes or no, thought Lewis. That's all she wants. Answer!

But it was an impossible question. If he said yes, everyone would laugh. Lewis Dearborn, an athlete? Ha, ha. If he said no, it would make him a weirdo. Lewis Dearborn doesn't like sports? It must be because he's so *special*.

He said nothing.

Finally, it was over.

On the long walk home, Lewis had time to think. Not about school—there was no point. He thought about the tower instead. How fantastic it had been, living there. In those first days upstairs, he'd been sure that nothing at school could touch him—not if he could go home to Libertalia. And now, instead, he'd go home to *more* impossible questions, this time from his parents and Mrs. Binchy. Did you have a good day? Did you have fun with your friends?

Why couldn't the pirates just leave him alone? Why couldn't they hang out somewhere else, as they had done when he first moved in? All he'd had to worry about then were a few noises.

He could *handle* noises.

His next thought stopped him in his tracks. What if the pirates *weren't* in the tower? What if he was avoiding Libertalia for nothing? There'd been no sign of them when he went upstairs with his father. Was it possible that the pirates had left?

Longing swept through Lewis like a tidal wave.

He turned into the Shornoway drive. There it was—the tower. He stared till his eyes began to water from the wind. Then he decided.

He was going back upstairs.

9

Y es!
They were gone.

Lewis had done a complete inspection, sniffing and searching the whole tower room, including under the beds. He'd even checked behind the red door. Everything was just as it should be. The air was fresh and sweet. The only sound was the sea.

"Yes!" he said out loud, pumping his fist in the air.

Looking around, he thought about what to do next. That was easy . . .

Anything he wanted!

He practiced handstands against the wall with his shoes *on*. He drew a time-traveling submarine and named it the *Atlanticus* and attached it to the wall with tacks. He took the tin soldiers out of the cabinet and lined them up in battle formation on his desk, reds against blues, using the stone and shell collections as landscape.

He even had dinner upstairs. His parents were out, and Mrs. Binchy let him bring his lasagna up on a tray. As he ate, he wondered whether his parents might let him have a TV up here.

The answer came immediately.

Not a chance.

"We don't believe in technology," his mother always said when he asked about TVs, tablets, electronic games, smart phones—anything, in fact, that had a battery or a plug.

"We don't think it's good for you," said his father. "We don't believe it's healthy for a developing mind."

The result was that Lewis's house had one TV (old, small) and two computers (his mother's laptop and the old desktop in his father's study). Even these were rationed. Seven hours a week of "screen time" was what Lewis was allowed, except when he was working on school projects.

It was medieval, that's what it was. And it was one more way for Mr. and Mrs. Dearborn to make their son weird. It was like they were *trying*!

His piece of lasagna was huge, but he wolfed down every bite. Afterward, he walked to the middle window. Opening it as wide as it would go, he leaned way out, inhaling the air in deep sucking gulps. It was as if he'd been holding his breath the whole time he'd been away.

And then he felt it. That slight drop in temperature. Coming from *behind*.

"The lad's back!" roared a familiar voice, so close Lewis felt the spray on his cheek. Crawley's battered face loomed into view. "I *knew* he'd not let us down. Didn't I say so, Skittles?"

Lewis whirled to face them.

"Aye," agreed Skittles, emerging from his cloud.

The others were showing themselves, too. "The lad's back, aye, he's back."

"I can smell him," snarled Jack the Rat, pushing through to sniff at Lewis. "He smells like fear!"

It was true. Fear snaked up Lewis's spine like an electric eel. He had forgotten how it felt to be closed in by these ghostly shapes, with their bizarre faces and pungent smells. His leg muscles tensed, ready to run.

The only thing that stopped him was the voice in his head. It told him that if he left now, he'd never come back.

Trembling, he held his ground. His fingers clutched the windowsill behind him.

"Now *that's* the spirit!" Crawley clapped with delight. "Look at him, clinging there like a barnacle. He'll be a grand help, he will."

The captain did a strange little dance, leaping about as if his boots were on fire. It was like a signal to the others, who began cheering and smacking each other on the backs.

Lewis stared in shock. They were celebrating! They thought he'd come back to *help* them.

"Enough!" yelled Crawley. He turned to Lewis. "What's the plan, lad? I likes a good plan!"

"Aye, tell us the plan!" echoed the others. They crowded in close, waiting for Lewis to speak.

For a moment, it was like being in school. Lewis felt his throat tighten. Then he remembered—they were adults. He was used to talking to adults. And they weren't even *real* adults.

"I don't . . . don't have a plan," he said, his voice barely a whisper. Then, seeing their faces cloud over, he added, "Not yet!"

"Not yet?" Crawley took a moment to consider this. "Well, that's fine." He squinted at Lewis with his good eye. "But when?"

"I don't know!" blurted Lewis. "I have to think!"

"Think?" shouted Jack the Rat. "What's the use of *thinking*?"

"Hssst, Jack!" hissed the captain. "It's good the lad is pondering it out. We doesn't want a half-cooked plan, does we?"

Jack grimaced and scratched his armpit.

Lewis's body stood rigid, but his mind raced. What if he *could* come up with a plan? One that would get the pirates to their ship all on their own? Without involving him?

He could get rid of them for good!

An idea flickered. "Wait here," he said. "I'll be right back."

The pirates shifted to let him through. He raced downstairs and shuffled through a magazine rack. Seconds later, he was back.

"Here," he said. "A map. It's Tandy Bay. I can show you a way that avoids most of the traffic." Opening the map, he held it out to Crawley.

Crawley glanced over, then crossed his arms. "That's of no use, lad."

"Why not?" asked Lewis. "I could mark it for you. Show you the whole route."

The other pirates gathered to examine the map.

"Lookee there," said Moyle. "All them words."

"So many of 'em," said Jonas.

"Too many!" muttered Jack.

Lewis pointed. "See? Here's the town hall and—"

"Didn't I *tell* you the lad could read?" Moyle smiled proudly at the others. "Talks like a book, don't he?"

The others nodded, impressed.

Suddenly, Lewis got it. "You mean . . . you can't read?"

The pirates laughed.

"Now where would we be learning that?" asked Skittles. "Us that had to earn our way from the age of—well, I were five when I were orphaned. Lived by my wits in the streets of Liverpool."

"I worked like a dog from the day I were weaned," said Moyle. "Looking after me dear sick mother. The two of us in the poorhouse."

"Poorhouse were a palace," muttered Jonas, "beside the life of a slave."

Lewis gaped. "You were a slave?"

Jonas nodded, his face grim. "Captured as a boy and packed into a ship that were no more than a traveling coffin. Took me to a plantation on an island off Jamaica, where the master—you never met such a devil! Except for maybe that Captain Dire what drowned us. As soon as I were old enough, I ran away. Joined up with some buccaneers and went to sea. Since then, I been free in body and soul."

"Not as free as you'd be in Libertalia," Moyle put in.

"Aye." Jonas heaved a sigh. "Libertalia. There ain't no such freedom as you find there."

"Libertalia?" Excitement coursed through Lewis. "You mean it's . . . a real place?"

"Why, o' course it is!" grinned Moyle. "Best place in the world for a pirate. Off the coast of Africa, on a sunny isle called Madagascar."

"It'd be *warm* there," said Jonas.

Lewis nodded. "I know about Madagascar."

"That's where Libertalia be," said little Skittles. "A kingdom of pirates where all is equal."

"Where they lives in peace and harmony," added Adam. "Where no man is better than another."

Crawley hoisted a tankard in a toast. "To Libertalia!" he shouted.

"To Libertalia!" echoed the others, raising their own tankards—where had those mugs come from?— and putting them to their lips to drink.

Was there anything *in* the tankards? wondered Lewis.

Crawley let out a disgustingly complicated belch. "Now, laddie. Back to the matter at hand. Our ship. What's the plan?"

Lewis sighed. He folded the map. If they couldn't read, it was useless. So much for his plan.

But the pirates were still staring. Waiting.

He had to give them *something*.

"You . . . well, you'd have to go at night," he said. He

was careful not to say "we." No way he was going there *with* them.

"Aye," said Moyle, nodding wisely. "Night would be best, for certain."

"And you should be . . . um, extremely quiet."

"True," rumbled Bellows. "Well said, lad."

"And, of course," added Lewis, gaining confidence, "you'd have to stay invisible."

He waited for agreement. To his surprise, they glanced away. Several twitched or bit their lips.

"What's wrong?" asked Lewis.

"Ah," said Crawley sadly, "if it were only that easy. But here's the rub, lad. A ghost may *make* hisself invisible, as you say. But he cannot guarantee to *keep* hisself that way. If something were to happen as to get us excited—why, we'd be as visible as you. Seen by anyone who cared to look!"

"It's the getting excited," added Skittles. "Makes us bright as ships' lanterns."

"Aye, and when we sees them things that go so fast, we gets *terrible* excited," said Jonas, breathing hard at the thought. As Lewis stared, he *did* seem to grow a little brighter.

"It's like when . . . when . . ." struggled Bellows. "Now what's that word for when your skin comes up red?"

"Blushing?" said Lewis.

"Aye, that's it." Bellows looked impressed by Lewis's cleverness. "When we gets excited, we comes up brighter, the way a lad like you might come up blushing."

Moyle leaned in close to Lewis, inspecting his face. "Lookee here, mates. The lad's blushing right now."

"I am not!" Lewis twisted away in embarrassment. He couldn't believe he was blushing *here!* With the pirates.

"It's all right," murmured Adam to the others. "He can't help it, no more than we can."

Lewis forced himself to concentrate. If the pirates were right—if they became visible when they got excited—then that changed everything. Invisible, they might make it across town, even past the police station. But visible? Looking the way they did? Not a chance.

He spoke carefully. "That'll make it . . . harder. I'll . . . I'll have to think about it."

"Think?" yelled Jack. "*More* thinking? I say we puts the thumbscrews to him. See how he likes a taste of—"

"Stow that talk!" interrupted Crawley. "If the lad says he must think, then that's what he must do. We'll just settle ourselves to wait."

With a flourish of his coattails, he claimed the wicker chair, while the others found places around the room. Everyone fell silent.

Lewis stood it for twenty seconds.

"I can't!" he said.

"Can't what?" said Crawley.

"Can't think with all of you watching me."

Crawley looked surprised. "You wants us to leave?"

"Well," said Lewis, "if you don't mind. Just for a while. So I can think."

Jack spat on the floor in disgust.

But Crawley just smiled. "Why didn't you say so, lad? We can disappear. Nothing easier."

"Really?" said Lewis. "Thank you."

They began to fade immediately. Emboldened by success, Lewis called, "Wait!"

They paused, and Lewis was treated to the fascinating sight of seven transparent bodies.

"I don't know if I can figure out a good plan right away," he told them. "I might have to come here in the afternoons . . . to think! It might take a while."

"Not to worry." Crawley was now barely an outline. "We's waited this long, hasn't we, mates? We has lots of time, we has."

"All the time in the world," added Moyle's voice from an empty spot near the desk.

Lewis covered his mouth to hide his delight. He could barely believe his luck. To think that he could come here tomorrow. And the next day. And the next.

He had done it.

Libertalia was *his* again.

10

At the end of the second week of school, a new girl turned up in Lewis's class. Seeing her walk in, Lewis felt a wave of relief. The more the kids noticed her, the less they would notice *him*. She had a strange name, Abriella, and a mother who was, if possible, even more embarrassing than his own.

"Sorry we're late," puffed the mother, bending over Ms. Forsley's desk so that her large blue-jeaned backside faced the class. "We've been on a bus for *five days*, can you believe it? All the way from the west coast."

Hearing a giggle, the mother turned. There it was—the thing the kids had spotted as she entered. A bare midriff and, right in the middle, her *belly button,* hanging out for the whole world to see, between rolls of fat. And, worse, it was pierced with a bellybutton *ring*!

Off to one side stood Abriella in a long green dress. She was odd, too, but in a completely different way. Skinny and long-legged, she'd be easily the tallest kid in sixth grade. Big eyes, almost pop-eyed. Long nose. Mouth so wide, the corners had to turn up in a smile even though she had absolutely nothing to smile about. Not with *that* mother.

The mother was telling Ms. Forsley her life story—how she'd married "a real zero," moved across the country, gotten a divorce, lost her "crappy job in a florist shop." It seemed she'd never stop.

"We're staying with my folks now, just till I get on my feet."

The woman wasn't Lewis's mother, but even so, he felt like going la-la-la in his head. He peeked at Abriella again. Chin tilted up, she was meeting the eyes of each new classmate in turn. Suddenly she was looking at—him! Not just *at* him. Through him! With those giant eyes. It was like being x-rayed. He glanced down, mortified.

After the mother left, Ms. Forsley said the usual things about making the new girl feel welcome.

"You can sit here, Abriella." She pointed to the desk in front of Lewis.

"Abbie," said the girl firmly as she sat down. "With an 'i-e.' Abbie."

At recess, everyone watched her. Lewis watched, too, uneasy, waiting for her to make mistakes. But she wandered the schoolyard with a loose, easy stride, an occasional cheery bounce punctuating her steps. Everywhere she went, she talked. Lewis was surprised—shocked even—at the way she talked to anyone at all. First-graders. Boys. Mrs. Reber. He couldn't hear what she said, but they all answered. When she reached the swings, she dropped into one and began pumping, her skirt riding up to show thin bare legs and scuffed black boots, higher and higher till she was almost even with the top frame. A sixth-grader, on a swing! When Mrs. Reber scolded her—the playground was crowded, she could hit someone— she just grinned. "Sorry," she yelled, dragging her feet to slow herself down.

Lewis was so busy watching, he didn't hear Seth approach.

"That your girlfriend, Dearborn?"

The boys in white laughed.

"Oh, wait, I forgot. You have to *talk* to get a girl-friend. Even a weird one like that."

Lewis swallowed. He opened his mouth to say—he didn't know what. Nothing came out.

"Duh," said Seth. "Come on, Lewisssssser, you can say it. Duh! Your mouth's already open."

More laughter.

"How about 'Ma-ma'? I bet you can say 'Ma-ma.'"

Lewis felt heat shoot through his body. Luckily, at that moment, Mrs. Reber strolled by. The boys in white scattered.

Lewis looked up. Abbie's swing had stopped. She was staring at him—at his tomato face.

He ran inside.

There was another surprise waiting for Lewis that day—when he got home from school. His father was wearing an apron! A giant white chef's apron, crisp and new.

It wasn't a total surprise. More and more, when Lewis came home, he'd been finding his father in an odd place—the messy, cluttered kitchen. Mr. Dearborn, it seemed, was helping Mrs. Binchy cook. How this had come about, Lewis didn't know. But the first time he saw his father bent over a cutting board, he could hardly believe his eyes. His father *never* cooked.

Seeing Lewis's face now, Mr. Dearborn waggled the knife he was holding above a pile of chopped walnuts. "Just making myself useful," he said cheerily.

Lewis glanced around. Mrs. Binchy was stirring a huge, steaming pot on the ancient stove. Her cat Patsy lay curled on a stack of newspapers. Fiddle music blared from a radio on the counter, half hidden under a pile of potato peels, while from the oven rose a rich baking smell.

Mrs. Binchy held out a wooden spoon. "Have a taste, dear. It's chowder."

Lewis blinked in surprise. She was offering him the spoon from the pot. He *never* ate from the pot spoon. It was unsanitary. His mother said so.

But his mother wasn't there. She was teaching. She wouldn't be home till six.

"Go on," said Mrs. Binchy, pushing the spoon at him.

Lewis glanced at his father. Mr. Dearborn grinned.

Obediently, Lewis took a slurp. The chowder was rich and creamy, thick with potatoes and seafood. He closed his eyes in wonder. Like everything Mrs. Binchy cooked, it was the best he'd ever tasted.

"There," said Mrs. Binchy. "I knew you'd like it. Want to help?"

"I . . . um, homework," said Lewis.

"Here," she said, "take a cheesy biscuit." She handed him two, still warm from the oven.

Biscuits in hand, he headed up to Libertalia.

He was feeling more at home in the tower room all

the time. The pirates had kept their word about leaving him alone. Every day after school, he climbed the stairs to Libertalia and stayed till dinnertime. And what did he do there? Anything. Everything. Whatever he wanted. There was neither a whiff nor a whisper from the ghosts.

And because they were so quiet, there was only one thing Lewis *didn't* do during his time in Libertalia. He didn't think about the pirates. Not once.

It wasn't that difficult, really.

Lewis was good at *not* thinking about things.

11

Several weeks later, on a dull, wet Thursday, Lewis's parents went out to a special dinner at his mother's college. It happened to be Mrs. Binchy's night off.

"We'll hire a babysitter," said Mrs. Dearborn.

"What?" said Lewis. "No! Please! Nobody my age has babysitters. Kids my age *are* babysitters."

His mother rolled her eyes. What *other* kids did, she said, was no concern of hers.

Mrs. Binchy came to the rescue. "Not to worry, Mrs. Dearborn. I'll be home early, eight at the latest. And, really, it's as peaceful as the grave out here."

Reluctantly, Mrs. Dearborn agreed.

"Keep the doors *locked*," she told Lewis, as she and

Mr. Dearborn left for dinner. She was wearing her shoes with the buckles instead of the ones with the laces. For her, Lewis knew, that was dressing up.

"You have my number," she said. "And if you have to call the fire or police—"

"Nine-one-one," said Lewis. How stupid could he be not to know *that*?

As soon as they left, he headed upstairs and stretched out on the brass bed. It was just quarter to five, and he thought he might read for a while before eating the casserole Mrs. Binchy had left in the oven. Soon he was deep into a novel about two boys lost in the Amazon rain forest. Snakes, giant insects, piranhas . . .

When his skin prickled, he thought it was just the danger in the book. Then he glanced up.

Seven dead pirates were gathered around his bed.

He let out a scream!

The pirates let out a few good screeches themselves. Most of them glowed several shades brighter.

"It's true!" cried Lewis, once he'd caught his breath.

"What? What?" demanded Crawley, looking rattled. "Speak, boy!"

"It's true that you get brighter when you're upset."

"*Who's* upset?" hollered Jack, shaking his fist. "Why, I'll—"

"Sssst!" ordered Crawley. He raised his eyebrows at Lewis. "Well?"

The others smiled expectantly.

"Oh," said Lewis, looking around. "I guess you're here about . . ."

"Aye!" said Crawley. "The plan!"

Lewis felt a stab of guilt. "It's not *quite* ready," he said. "I'm . . . I'm working on it."

"Aye." Crawley nodded happily. "We sees you sitting here, day after day, dreaming up schemes. I'm sure it will be a *grand* plan, what with all this thinking."

"Pah!" said Jack.

"Well . . ." said Lewis, suddenly eager to leave. He closed his book and scrambled off the bed.

But Moyle stepped forward, blocking his way. "Why, lookee here, Captain! See this great thick book the lad holds? As easy for him as climbing a mast. I *told* you he could read to us."

Lewis held his breath. What now?

"Aye," agreed Captain Crawley. "Doubtless, he can. Adam! Fetch the book."

Adam ran to the glass cabinet. He held up a book. "This one?"

"No," said Bellows. "It were red."

Adam searched again. "This?"

"No, it were smaller," said Skittles. Pushing past

Adam, he reached for a shabby red book. "Here it be!"

He thrust it in Lewis's face. "Read!"

Lewis peered, dumbfounded, at the cover. *Peter and Wendy*, it said in letters so faded they were almost indecipherable. He thought for a moment. "Peter Pan?"

"Aye," chorused the pirates. "Peter Pan." They sank, one by one, to the floor and gazed raptly up at him. Looking down, Lewis thought that—except for their age and filthy clothes and missing body parts—they could have been a storytime group in a library.

Tentatively, he opened the book.

"Read!" demanded Crawley.

"I'm not . . . very good at reading aloud," said Lewis. "Usually I just—"

"Read!"

Lewis took a deep breath and began. "All . . . all children, except one, grow up. They soon know that they will grow up, and the way Wendy knew—"

"No!" said Moyle. "Not that! Find where it tells about Captain Hook!"

"Aye," said the others. "Give us Hook!"

Lewis tried to explain. "It's not that easy. You can't just open a book to—"

Jack leaped to his feet. "FIND CAPTAIN HOOK!" he roared, his hand on the hilt of his sword.

"I'll try," said Lewis quickly. He leafed through the book, checking pages at random. Finally, he spotted the word "Hook." As he began to read, growls of appreciation drifted up from the floor.

And so he read about Captain Hook and the crocodile who had swallowed Hook's hand and then followed him around, waiting for the rest. Moving through the paragraphs, Lewis couldn't help peeking at his own pirates, with their various missing bits. No wonder they were fascinated by Hook.

He read on, losing track of time, losing track of himself, hypnotized, like the pirates, by the story and the sound of his own voice. Whenever the book drifted to other characters—Peter, the Lost Boys, Wendy—the pirates grew impatient. "HOOK! HOOK!" they cried, forcing him to search again.

"Ah, that were a treat," said Crawley finally, with a deep sigh. "You reads like a charm, young Lewis. Near as good as your great-granddaddy."

"Great-Granddad read to you?"

"Aye, when he were about your age. He read us about Hook many a time."

And, indeed, Lewis had noticed that in certain parts, the pirates' lips had moved in unison with his. They had actually *memorized* sections.

"I wish we'd met this Hook," said Moyle, "but in all

our sailing of the seven seas, we never come across him."

"Well, no," said Lewis, "you couldn't. He's—"

He was going to say "not real," but stopped. The pirates, still in the grip of the story, had a strange contented light in their eyes. It would be like telling a five-year-old there was no tooth fairy.

He closed the book instead.

"I . . . I have to go now," he said. "Dinner."

At the door, he looked back. They were sitting where he'd left them.

"What are you going to do now?" he asked.

Crawley grinned crookedly. "No way of knowing, lad. But you've put us in a fine way to make a grand evening of it. Hasn't he, boys?"

"Aye!" cried Bellows. "We'll shake the floor tonight, by thunder."

Lewis waited. *Shake the floor?* But no explanation was offered. He left.

The macaroni and cheese was dry, but still tasty. Lewis ate it standing at the counter. Afterward, he washed and dried his dishes.

Then he headed for the spare room where he'd been sleeping, even though he still didn't think of it as "his" room. The bins and boxes were gone now, but his mother's sewing machine still sat like a lump in the corner. The couch, made up neatly into a bed, looked as if it were awaiting a paying guest.

Lewis walked to the window and tried to raise it, but it was stuck. He made a few more efforts, grunting. Then he stared at the empty driveway.

What were they *doing* upstairs?

His toes began to tap. Slowly. Nervously. Then faster. He ran for the back staircase.

He only meant to take a peek. He only wanted to satisfy his curiosity.

But when he saw what looked like a party, when he heard the shouts to "Come in, lad!" he couldn't stop himself. Soon he was perched on the edge of the brass bed, watching what appeared to be a card game— except that Lewis had never seen cards played so *actively* before. Skittles, Moyle and Jonas squatted tensely in a circle, slamming down cards with such force that Lewis couldn't help jumping. The rules were unclear, but there seemed to be a lot of shoving and whacking across the head, neither of which Lewis had ever imagined to be part of a card game.

Across the room, Adam was playing a small metal flute for Jack and Barnaby Bellows, who were dancing a kind of jig. Mostly this consisted of hopping from one foot to the other with ferocious energy, but occasionally the partners seized one another and spun in a frenzied circle. The floor, Lewis noticed, actually *did* shake as Bellows's huge feet pounded the boards.

Crawley stood back, but his damaged face had an air of deep contentment. It wasn't long before he burst into song:

Come, ye young sailors with spirits bold.
We'll venture forth in search of gold.
Way hay, let the winds blow,
There's forty fathoms and more below.

Here, other voices joined in:

And if we drown while we are young,
Better we drown than e'er be hung.
Way hay, let the winds blow,
There's forty fathoms and more below.

Nail the black flag to the mast,
We're Libertalia bound at last.
Way hay, let the winds blow,
There's forty fathoms and more below.

The captain hoisted his tankard. "To the *Maria Louisa!*"

The others clinked their mugs before glugging the contents down. At least, they *appeared* to be glugging.

Lewis couldn't stand it any longer. He whispered a question to Skittles.

"No," said Skittles morosely. "We can't drink a drop and we can't eat nothing, neither, more's the pity. We tried at first, but it just went right through us."

"Now we pretends," said Jonas, overhearing. "But it ain't the same. Oh, what I wouldn't give for a pint of grog."

"I'd give me right arm," said Skittles. "If I had one."

Out of the corner of his eye, Lewis noticed that Adam had wandered over to the onyx chess set. He was picking up a pawn.

Lewis was about to say "Stop!" but something in Adam's face made him catch himself. Joining the cabin boy, he whispered, "Do you know how to play?"

Adam shook his head.

"Would you like to learn?"

A huge crooked smile was Lewis's answer.

And that's how it happened that, twenty minutes later, the two boys—human and ghost—were engaged in a head-to-head chess game. The other pirates gathered to watch and to shout encouragement to the cabin boy, along with ridiculous suggestions. The entire audience was on Adam's side, and at first this bothered Lewis. But then he told himself that Adam was new to the game and lacking in confidence. Adam *needed* fans.

Still, Lewis couldn't help being unsettled by their reaction when Adam lost. The pirates howled their disapproval, waving their pistols and accusing Lewis of cheating. Jack threatened to give him twenty lashes.

"No!" cried Adam, his eyes shining. "Lewis won, fair and square. It were a grand game, and . . ."

He stared at Lewis, hesitating.

"Yes?" said Lewis.

"Might I make so bold, sir, as to ask for another?"

Lewis had never been called *sir* before.

"Uh . . . okay," he said.

They played another game, and Lewis won again. This time he wasn't *quite* so flustered when the pirates hollered at him.

"Another?" begged Adam.

Lewis nodded, then realized how late it must be. "I'll be right back," he said and ran down to the kitchen.

Mrs. Binchy was home. He could tell by the warm teapot on the counter and the TV sounds from her room. How lucky she hadn't come looking for him! He found a piece of paper and wrote:

Dear Mom and Dad and Mrs. Binchy,

I'm going to sleep upstairs in the tower room.
Please don't worry. I brushed my teeth and took
my vitamins.

Goodnight, sleep tight, don't let the bedbugs bite!

Your son (and friend),
Lewis

He put the note on the kitchen table and weighed it down with the pepper grinder. He brushed his teeth. He took his vitamins.

Then he ran back up to Libertalia.

12

The party, if that's what it was, went on most of the night. Lewis lost track of time. At some point, he fell into a fitful sleep, interrupted periodically by shouts or singing. The pirates never seemed to get sleepy. Then again, thought Lewis, why would they?

He opened his eyes to an empty room, sunlight pouring through the tall windows. The only sound was the ringing of the kitchen bell—Mrs. Binchy, telling him he was late. He stumbled downstairs.

At school, he had to keep blinking himself awake. In the middle of social studies, chin resting on his fists, he actually fell asleep.

The word "Shornoway" woke him. Ms. Forsley was talking about historic buildings in Tandy Bay, and Shornoway was one of them. She named others, too— the doctor's office, Stellars Grocery Store. Lewis realized that this must be part of the "local history" they were going to study. He forced his eyes open.

But at afternoon recess, crouched and leaning against the back wall of the school, he fell again into a doze.

"Hey, look at this!" Seth's voice. "Lewisser's gone sleepy-bye."

Lewis burrowed his chin into his jacket. Ostrich, he told himself.

"Nice hair!" said Seth. "Maybe we can make it even nicer . . ."

Other voices laughed. The boys in white.

Before Lewis could move, something rubbed hard across the top of his head. A sharp sweet odor filled the air.

He jumped up, grabbing his head. Perfume! Seth had smeared perfume in his hair.

He looked around. The boys in white had bolted. But Seth was still there, wagging a foil packet—the kind that comes free in the mail.

"It's called *Sweet Dreams*," he said. "Smells good on you, Dearborn."

Lewis ran for the washroom and straight into a cubicle. He hid there till he was sure the room was empty. Then he washed his hair, sticking his head in a sink and using the pink liquid soap.

After recess, Ms. Forsley sniffed the air. She said she didn't know who was using perfume, but whoever it was, she would like them to stop because some people, including her, were allergic.

Lewis twisted his pencil in his fingers until it snapped. Bite marks mottled the yellow paint.

Abbie's hand slowly reached back toward him. It dropped a folded paper on his desk. He opened it.

Something stinks in this class, and it's not perfume.

He read it again.

Was she talking about *him*? Was she saying *he* stunk? Maybe he smelled musty, like Shornoway. Or worse, like the pirates. That dead-fish smell.

For the rest of the day, he barely moved, showing nothing. He sat so stiffly, his neck hurt.

When he got home, his father and Mrs. Binchy were in the kitchen. Mr. Dearborn was up to his wrists in dough.

"Torta rustica!" he called. "I've been eager to try it."

"Your father has the knack," added Mrs. Binchy. "It's a gift!"

Lewis took a closer look at his father, and his heart sank. Mr. Dearborn was wearing a *hairnet.*

And bad as that was, it was just part of a much bigger craziness. His father was now collecting cookbooks. Huge, heavy ones you could hardly lift. He'd brought home a crepe pan, too—from France—and a stock pot so big it barely fit on the stove. He and Mrs. Binchy were making way too much food, and the freezer was filling with leftovers no one could eat. It was like that fairy tale about the porridge pot that overflows till the whole town is swamped.

As Lewis left the kitchen, he thought, not for the first time, that it was no wonder he wasn't normal. How *could* he be?

He stood under a hot shower for fifteen minutes, scrubbing his hair, then used his father's deodorant afterward. At dinner, he discovered that torta rustica was a kind of vegetable pie. It didn't *sound* good, but the taste was amazing. Everyone had large helpings. Even so, they barely made a dent in the enormous pie.

"And where are you sleeping tonight?" asked his father. "Seeing as you seem to have two bedrooms now?"

Before Lewis could answer—he actually wasn't sure how he *would* answer—his mother broke in.

"For goodness sake, Lewis, must you slouch? You'll ruin your spine that way."

He jerked up straight in his chair. "The tower," he told his father in a firm voice. *"That's* where I sleep."

Upstairs, the pirates were waiting in their story-time circle. Skittles clutched the book.

"HOOK!" they chanted, as Lewis walked in. "HOOK! HOOK! HOOK!"

He read for most of an hour, searching, as before, for the pages that featured Captain Hook. These weren't always easy to find, and the pirates grew impatient while he looked. Not only that, he was already repeating the same bits.

"Excuse me," he said finally. "I don't mind reading. But maybe . . . could we find another book?"

His audience erupted in shouts. "Stow it! No! We likes Hook!"

"Silence!" cried Crawley. "What book does you mean?"

Lewis gulped. "Well, there are other pirate books. What about . . ." He thought quickly. *"Treasure Island?"*

The pirates looked blank.

"Now what might that be?" asked Crawley.

Lewis stared back in surprise. He'd never read *Treasure Island* himself, but he knew it was a classic. "Great-Granddad didn't read *Treasure Island* to you?"

"Not a word! But I likes the name. Does it have a treasure?"

Lewis nodded. "I think so."

"Doubloons?" asked Jonas.

"Pieces of eight?" asked Skittles.

"Louis d'ors and guineas?" asked Bellows.

"Probably," said Lewis, although he wasn't even sure what those words meant. Coins, he guessed, recognizing "pieces of eight."

"What say you, mates?" Crawley glanced around. "After all these years, might we be ready for a new book?"

"*I* am!" cried Adam.

"I likes the *old* book," snarled Jack, fingering his knife.

"Done!" said Crawley, ignoring Jack. "The lad will begin tomorrow to read us his new book about the treasure."

"But I don't even have—" began Lewis.

"Tomorrow!" ordered Crawley.

At lunch the next day, Lewis went to the school library to look for *Treasure Island*. He found an old hardcover copy and flipped through. It wasn't funny, like *Peter Pan*, but it *did* have pirates.

Hearing a familiar voice, he turned. Abbie was sitting at the next table with Leticia and Katy from his class. They were waiting for lunchtime book club.

Staring at the open pages of *Treasure Island*, he listened in.

They were talking about Abbie's scarf, a silvery one

with feathery bits at the ends. Leticia and Katy liked it, which surprised Lewis. He had noticed it, too, and thought it was weird.

But the real surprise was that Leticia and Katy were with Abbie at all. Abbie had only been there two weeks, and she had the world's most embarrassing mother. How had she made friends already?

But, of course, *she* talked. She knew what to say to other kids. Lewis could see that that was a big help.

She was talking now. "It's from the thrift store."

"What?" said Leticia. "You mean, Rag Time?"

Lewis held his breath. He had heard girls talk about Rag Time. They said it was full of old ladies and poor people. They said it stunk.

"Uh-huh," said Abbie. "It's not a fancy place, but it has some fantastic stuff."

A long silence.

"Really?" said Leticia.

"I found a charm bracelet there, too. Sterling silver. Antique. It has charms from all over—a Hawaiian dancer, a kangaroo. I'll bring it tomorrow."

Lewis waited.

"The scarf really *is* pretty," said Katy.

"Come *with* me," said Abbie. "To Rag Time. Bring five bucks. You'll be shocked."

Lewis waited for it. The "Ewww!"

"Okay," said Katy after a moment. "Sure."

"Me, too," said Leticia a moment later.

Lewis glanced up in amazement. Abbie's mouth, wide at any time, took over her whole face as she grinned at him.

What was she? A hypnotist? She'd convinced the two most popular girls in the class to go to the *thrift store* with her!

Later that day, in math class, he got groggy—and no wonder. The pirates had had another party, making sleep impossible. He must have dozed off because when Ms. Forsley tapped his desk, he had no idea what she was talking about.

"Lewis? Are you having trouble with the assignment?"

He glanced around. The other kids were writing in their exercise books. His wasn't even open. Neither was his math book.

"Better get started," said Ms. Forsley. "We'll be going over it in ten minutes."

When she'd moved on, Abbie passed him a note.

Problems 1, 3 & 9 on page 51.

He stared at her thin back. One end of the silvery scarf hung down behind.

"Thanks," he whispered.

She gave a little wave.

He continued to stare in confusion. Why did she help him? And why had she smiled at him in the library? As if they were friends.

They weren't friends. He knew that.

But he was glad about the little note. And the scarf wasn't *that* bad. Now that he looked at it.

On the following Tuesday, Ms. Forsley clasped her hands and smiled. "I have the most wonderful surprise."

She looked so excited that Lewis tried to guess. What could be so wonderful in social studies class?

"Remember how we talked about historic buildings in Tandy Bay? Well, I've just learned that someone in our class lives in one of the oldest buildings of all. Shornoway! And *we're* going to have a chance to see it. Lewis's mother has invited us for a class visit. Shall we thank Lewis and his family?"

As Lewis sat dumbstruck, she began to clap! The kids, one by one, joined in.

"Now, Lewis," she said, beaming, "I hope *you'll* act as our guide. Living there every day, you must have discovered some great nooks and crannies. We'd love to explore them with you, wouldn't we, class?"

Some of the kids murmured yes. Abbie turned to smile.

Lewis's shock turned to horror.

His class? Touring Shornoway? All these kids, who *already* thought he was weird, coming to see the crumbling walls and boarded-up windows?

Shornoway looked like a haunted house. No, he corrected himself, it didn't *look* like a haunted house. It *was* a haunted house! Lewis lived in a haunted house, and his class was coming to visit.

Pictures flashed through his mind. His father in a hairnet. Mrs. Binchy in her dead-Fred slippers. Not to mention the pirates. Could he count on them to stay hidden? He only had to think for two seconds to realize that he couldn't count on the pirates for *anything*.

He had to stop the tour.

When his mother pulled into the driveway that night, he was waiting.

"Lewis?" she said, as she opened the car door. "Is something wrong?"

"No. Well, actually, yes! Ms. . . . uh, Ms. Forsley said today . . . about a class visit? Here? To Shornoway?"

His mother stepped out, hauling her heavy black briefcase. "Oh, right. I told her there wasn't much to see. But she's very keen. Belongs to the Historical Society. They love these old wrecks."

"Well," he went on, "couldn't you . . . couldn't you tell her again how wrecked it is? Tell her it's . . . unsafe! It *is* unsafe, you know. All this moldy air and . . . and dust. There are kids in my class who really *do* have asthma."

Mrs. Dearborn paused in the driveway to glower. "For heaven's sake, Lewis, *what* is your problem? Is there some reason you don't want your class to come here?"

Reason, thought Lewis. There are a *thousand* reasons! But all he could say was, "Well . . . the air."

"Nonsense," said his mother. "They'll only be here an hour or two. And they're not coming till the sixteenth. Ms. Forsley wanted to come this week, but I already have my hands full with the real estate agents."

"The—*what*?" said Lewis.

But his mother had moved inside. He had to run to keep up.

"What real estate agents? What are you talking about?"

She frowned as she hung up her coat. "What's gotten into you? The people who are going to sell Shornoway, of course. They're coming on Friday to look around."

"But," said Lewis, his heart pounding, "but . . . but why are they coming *now*? It's only October. We have to live here till February!"

His mother put her hand on his forehead. "Are you okay, Lewis? You look flushed. Have you been taking your vitamin C?"

"Mom, please! Why now?"

Mrs. Dearborn sighed. "We're getting things rolling, Lewis. Shornoway isn't just some ordinary house, you know. It's an unusual property. Unique. The agents will have to look for the right buyer and—"

"There you are!" Mr. Dearborn pushed through the kitchen door. "Perfect timing—dinner's on the table. Filo bake, with Brie and shitake mushrooms!"

And that was that. Once his father started talking about food, there was no competing.

But with their plates finally filled, Lewis managed to get in a question. "Will they be going everywhere?"

"Who?" said his mother.

"The real estate people. Will they be going all over the house? Like . . . up to the tower?"

"Of course," said Mrs. Dearborn, and then, "Oh, *I* see the problem. Don't worry, Lewis. I'll tell them not to touch your things."

Lewis opened his mouth, then closed it. There was nothing to say.

Later that evening, he snuck outside. He made his way to the top of the cliff path and crouched there in the fog, shivering and hugging his knees. Spray misted his face. Surf pounded the rocks below.

Real estate agents! This was even worse than the class visit. A whole new, terrible problem.

No, thought Lewis, being honest—it was actually an *old* problem. One he'd been refusing to think about. The real estate agents were bound to say *something* that would make it clear—even to the pirates, who were slow about such things—that Shornoway was going to be sold.

They didn't know! All these hours he'd spent with the pirates, and he'd never told them the truth. Thinking about it now, he felt sick. The pirates had lived in Shornoway since it was first built, and for all that time, the house had been owned by the same family. Lewis's family.

The worst part was . . . they were ready to leave. And *he* could have helped them. In fact, he had *promised* to help them. The famous "plan" they were waiting for.

A foghorn blew in the distance. Lewis rubbed his chilly arms. What had he been thinking? Had he really believed that, at the end of six months, he could just move out of Shornoway and leave the pirates behind? Without a word?

Now there was no choice. He'd have to tell them about the real estate agents who were going to sell Shornoway.

The moment *that* thought sunk in, he realized something else.

He would have to do what they asked. He racked his brain for a long time, searching for another answer, but in the end, there was none.

He would have to take them to their ship.

14

"I'll do it," said Lewis, with only a slight quiver in his voice. "Here's the plan. I'm going to take you to the museum myself. I'll make sure you don't run into cars. And we'll go soon."

There was a moment of silence as the pirates absorbed this—then wild pandemonium as they leaped around, crashing into furniture and punching one another's arms.

Watching them, Lewis was glad he'd decided to tell them the good news first.

"I *have* to take you because . . . because my parents are going to sell Shornoway."

It was like pricking a balloon. The pirates faded

and sagged.

"Sell the old manse?" repeated Crawley. "To who?"

"Strangers?" demanded Jack the Rat.

Lewis gulped. "I don't know. Yes, I guess, strangers. But you see, it won't matter because you'll be gone! You'll be on the *Maria Louisa*. Right?"

Without warning, his eyes pricked with tears. Suddenly, he could *see* the tower room—with strangers in it. No! He couldn't think about that.

He focused on the pirates, who were staring at one another uneasily.

"If there's going to be *strangers* living here in Libertalia," muttered Moyle, "it's right that we go soon. We doesn't take to strangers, lad."

"That's true," said Skittles in a quivery voice. "We ain't met a stranger in a good many years."

"But . . ." said Adam and stopped.

Lewis nodded encouragingly.

"Ain't there strangers out there in the world, too?" blurted the cabin boy. "On that road, like? And in that moo-see-um?"

Skittles winced, and his body brightened with alarm. The same thing happened to Bellows. Clearly they hadn't thought the whole thing through.

"We been here a long time," mumbled Jonas. "Safe, like."

Lewis swallowed hard. What now? After all this, was he now going to have to persuade them to leave?

Trying to hide his own anxiety, he said, "Don't worry. I'll be with you all the way."

"Well said!" Crawley whacked Lewis across the back. "Rest easy, mates. We has the lad! He knows *everything* about the world out there and all them strangers, too."

"Aye, we has the lad!" agreed Moyle, trying to smile.

"Name the hour, young Lewis," ordered Crawley. "We're ready."

"Well," said Lewis, "soon."

The sooner, the better, he thought. Before the real estate agents came. And his class.

"But . . ." He struggled to say it. "There's still a tiny problem."

"Problem?" Crawley fixed him with a belligerent eye.

"It's . . . it's the same as before," stammered Lewis. Suddenly, it all spilled out. "Captain Crawley, you just don't look like the people around here. You look like what you are. Pirates! Ghosts! You *have* to stay invisible when we go. All of you! If people see you, it'll be a disaster."

Worst of all, he thought, a disaster for *him*. He allowed himself to picture, just for an instant, what would happen if people in Tandy Bay spotted the

118

ghoulish pirate crew . . . and Lewis Dearborn walking among them. No! Lewis Dearborn *leading* them. His reputation as a weirdo would be sealed forever. He'd spend the rest of his life trying to explain.

"You have to stay invisible," he repeated.

Crawley slung an arm around Lewis's shoulders, pulling him aside. "Laddie," he whispered, "ain't you listening? Now, for myself, I ain't afeared of nothing. Not strangers. Not them things that go fast—"

"Cars," said Lewis.

"Cars," agreed Crawley. "But the boys? Well, you can see how it is for them. Just talking about it, they're going on and off like them things you puts in your lamps."

"Lightbulbs," said Lewis.

"Aye! They're glowing and dimming like lightbulbs. And we ain't even left the house." Crawley clutched Lewis tighter. "So you see, lad . . . we has to find a way to get there *visible*."

Lewis swayed, feeling faint. It was impossible. Even if they snuck out at night, even if they only ran into one Tandy Bay resident, it would be a nightmare. Lewis pictured a late-night shift worker fleeing in terror, yelling into his cell phone at the 911 operator: "Yes, that's right! LEWIS DEARBORN! He's the leader!"

Suddenly, Crawley let out a whoop. "Son of a sea biscuit!" he yelled. "I knows! By all the saints and sinners, I *knows* how to do it."

"Wh-what?" said Lewis, as the other pirates gathered around. "How?" He was drowned out by shouts.

"Garments!" hollered Crawley above the din. "Ah, mateys, it's a lucky thing we have the lad—and him knowing all about what folks wears nowadays. Give a cheer now! For the lad!"

"Huzzah!" yelled the pirates. "Huzzah for the lad!"

Alarm bells clanged wildly in Lewis's head. "Me? What do you—"

"Here's the plan again, a mite improved," interrupted Crawley. "We needs to look like *travelers,* lad! We needs to appear as ordinary traveling folks passing through the village."

Lewis blinked. "You want to pass as . . . tourists?"

"Tourists! Aye, that'd be it. You needs to dress us up, laddie, in clothing such as *tourists* would wear. Mayhap we'll be lucky and no one will see us. But if we is seen, lad, we needs to look like a crew of ordinary tourists."

He grinned, the gaps in his smile winking darkly. His good eye blinked, while the other stayed fixed in a frozen stare.

Tearing his gaze away, Lewis looked around the

rest of the group. At Jonas's missing fingers. At the scar that carved Moyle's forehead in two. At Jack's hunched posture and lip-licking scowls.

The only one who was even close to normal-looking was Adam.

How could he make them look like modern tourists? It was insane!

And yet Crawley was right. They'd have to do something.

"I'm not really an expert on clothes," he said hesitantly. "I mean, of course I *have* clothes, and my dad does, too. But I don't know if they'll fit." He glanced at the colossal Bellows and the diminutive Skittles.

The pirates didn't reply.

"I don't have much money, either," he added, thinking out loud. "It would cost a lot to buy you . . . er, tourist outfits."

Moyle laughed. "No need for money. Easier just to *steal* 'em!"

"Aye!" growled Bellows. "Steal 'em. We'll show you how."

Lewis shrank back. "I can't do that!"

"Why not?" demanded Crawley. "Don't folks do laundry round here? Don't they hang it outdoors to dry? Why, it would be easy as drifting with the tide to steal some nice clean britches for me and the boys."

"People don't hang their laundry outside anymore," explained Lewis, "at least not this time of year. They have dryers mostly and . . ."

He stopped, overwhelmed by the enormity of it all.

Seeing the look on Lewis's face, Adam crept closer. "It don't have to be nothing fancy," he whispered.

Lewis shook his head, but the words "nothing fancy" triggered a memory. The conversation he had overheard at school. Abbie's scarf. He realized suddenly that he *did* know where to get clothes that weren't fancy—or expensive, either.

"The thrift store," he said under his breath.

"Beg pardon?" said Crawley.

"It's a place where they sell secondhand clothes. They're cheap. I could afford to buy you clothes there." Actually, he wasn't sure. He'd never been in Rag Time. He could only hope that his $37 in savings would be enough.

The pirates clapped and pounded the furniture, delighted by this new development.

"I ain't had new britches in hunnerts of years," said Bellows, looking down at his ragged pants, the color of mud. "I'd like some blue ones, I would. Might I go with you, lad, to that thrifty shop, to fetch 'em?"

"I'll go, too," grunted Jack. "I still doesn't trusssst the little bludger."

Skittles smiled timidly. "Well, if it ain't too far, I could—"

"No!" said Lewis. "I—"

"Back, you lubbers!" Crawley swatted Skittles across the back of the head. "The lad don't need *you* blocking his path out there. No! *I'll* go with him."

"What?" said Lewis.

Grabbing the boy's arm, Crawley pulled him aside again, out of hearing of the others. "Lookee here, lad. I been cooped up a long time, and I'm restless as a bat in a jar. I needs a peek at the world, I do."

"But—"

"You knows I can stay invisible, right? Won't be no problem for me."

"Well—"

"I could give you advice in your ear. About fittings and such."

Lewis thought quickly. He *was* a little nervous about picking out clothes. And the captain *was* an adult—of a sort. If Crawley could stay out of sight, he might actually be helpful.

"Okay," he said, before he could change his mind.

"When?" said Crawley.

"Tomorrow. After school."

"Tomorrow!" repeated Crawley, clapping his hands in excitement.

"Remember," said Lewis. "You promised."

"Promised what?"

"To stay invisible!"

"Aye, lad, of course. Do you think I wants to give meself grief? You won't see a hair of me. Not a hair."

"Okay," said Lewis. Exhausted, he dropped onto his bed and closed his eyes.

He might have fallen asleep, just like that, in all his clothes, except for the book that was placed gently on his right arm. He opened his eyes.

Treasure Island. He looked around. They were sitting on the floor, waiting.

He sighed. Sitting up, he opened the book.

The boy in this story was Jim Hawkins. And, like Lewis, he had found himself accidentally in the middle of a pirate crew. Lewis felt a real kinship to Jim, whose pirates were causing him huge amounts of risk and aggravation.

But that was where the similarities ended. Jim Hawkins was the kind of boy Great-Granddad had described—a "bold one," fearless and decisive. Jim would make things work. He was the kind of boy who solved problems.

But him? Lewis Dearborn?

One thing at a time, he told himself.

First, the clothes . . .

15

The next day, Lewis raced home from school. With barely a hello to his father, he charged straight up to Libertalia.

Twenty minutes later, he opened the front door of Shornoway and stepped outside. He was alone. But a sharp-eyed observer might have noticed that he was talking to an empty space just to his left.

"Excuse me, Captain Crawley," he was saying. "If we're going to walk all the way to the thrift store together, you're going to have to loosen up on my arm. You're making a bruise."

The vice-like grip on his left arm relaxed, then tightened again as they reached the street.

"Here comes one now! Watch out! CARRRR!" said the voice in his ear.

"Ow!" Lewis pulled away. "Captain Crawley, please. Just *look* at that car. See how it stays in its own lane? As long as we walk on the side, we're safe."

"By thunder, them things goes fast!" gasped Crawley. "Hold on now, laddie, while I catches me breath."

Lewis waited obediently, wondering whether it had been a mistake to bring Crawley. Peering in the captain's direction, he could make out a faint ghostly outline. Would Crawley be able to keep his promise?

"Maybe we should go back," he said.

"Never!" declared Crawley. "I weren't afeared of the evil Captain Dire, and I ain't afeared of them car things neither." To Lewis's relief, he faded.

"We'll be off this road soon," said Lewis. "Try to relax."

Muckanutt Road, where they were walking, was more like a small highway than a street. It had no sidewalks for pedestrians, just gravel shoulders. Shown as a "scenic route" on maps, it attracted plenty of tourist traffic. Lewis could understand why the pirates had been frightened.

He hurried along the shoulder now, his ghostly shadow keeping pace. All went well until a woman in a blue tracksuit ran out of her drive. Before Lewis had a chance to think, she charged straight at the place where Crawley was walking.

"Iiyy!" cried Lewis.

The woman stopped.

"Are you okay?" she asked, looking into Lewis's eyes. Her face showed concern, but no alarm. She had run right *through* Crawley! She hadn't even noticed!

"Fine," squeaked Lewis.

"Who's afeared now?" whispered the captain as the woman ran off.

"Well, *I* don't know how this stuff works. I thought she would—you know—hit you."

"Not if I'm invisible, lad. Not unless I wants her to."

"Well, how am *I* supposed to know that?" asked Lewis, thoroughly rattled.

Out of the corner of his eye, he noticed the bus stop across the street. Two old ladies in long coats huddled together on a bench, their feet not quite reaching the ground. They were pointing at Lewis and whispering.

"Oh, for Pete's sake!" said Lewis out loud, giving the old ladies even more reason to stare. He broke into a slow run, determined to get off Muckanutt Road before a bus came along. The captain stayed with him; Lewis could tell by the drag on his arm.

Things got better when they could finally turn onto Highbury Lane—a quiet street, almost deserted.

Following a route of back streets to the town center, they managed to avoid all but three cars, and those were moving slowly. Crawley's grip on Lewis's arm relaxed, but he still noticed every vehicle.

"What about this grand white carriage, lad?" He jerked Lewis to a stop beside a parked delivery van. "Would this be faster than the others?"

"Not really. Probably slower."

"Slower," marveled Crawley. "Fancy that!"

A kid on a skateboard caught Crawley's attention, then another on a bicycle. Everything had to be explained. It was as if the captain were from another planet. Thinking about this, Lewis realized that he actually *was* from another planet, in a way. The earth had been a different place back in Crawley's time.

Rag Time was on the busiest section of Front Street, so the last block was a challenge. When a car alarm went off, Crawley threw himself—and Lewis!— hard against a building. Lewis stifled a yell as he hit the bricks. Beside him, the ghostly outline appeared, then vanished. Luckily, the few pedestrians nearby didn't notice.

With his heart in his throat, Lewis opened the door to the thrift store.

"Thunderation!" The voice beside him spoke clearly, at a level far above the whisper they'd agreed on. "Look at the *size* of this place! All them garments, already sewed up! Where's the tailor?"

"Shhh!" hissed Lewis. "There *is* no tailor. Everything here was made in a factory."

"A factory! Now what would that be?"

"Shhh!" said Lewis again. "I'll explain later."

They were already attracting attention. The cashier, a puffy-haired woman in a mustard-colored sweatshirt, stared at Lewis, her mouth open. Lewis knew just how she felt. He'd felt the same way, years ago, watching Great-Granddad talk to himself.

He waved awkwardly at the cashier. "Just looking for . . . er, men's stuff."

She pointed.

"Thanks." Lewis swerved right, dragging Crawley behind him like an anchor.

The men's area consisted of a wall of suits and jackets, a round rack of shirts and several rows of hanging pants. The only other customer, a large woman in turquoise stretch pants, was examining a display of neckties.

Lewis headed for the shirts.

"The small sizes are on this end," he whispered to his invisible companion. "The big ones down there." He wasn't sure which direction to speak, now that Crawley had released his arm.

"OW!" said a female voice. Lewis turned.

The turquoise woman was storming toward him, cheeks mottled with anger. "Listen, kid! I do *not* find that funny!"

She pushed right up to him, nose to nose. She was practically breathing fire. "For two cents, I'd give you a wallop!"

Lewis could see individual eyelashes, thick with mascara.

"Sorry," he bleated.

The woman glared silently, then stalked away.

"Crawley?" whispered Lewis. "What did you *do*?"

A chuckle came into his ear. "Just a wee pinch. By the powers, she's a fine-looking woman."

"Crawley! *Stop that!* No more pinching. I mean it!"

"Aye, lad, you're right. We has work to do." Pairs of pants started rising off the racks.

"No!" whispered Lewis. "Just tell me which ones. *I'll* pick them up."

Quickly they worked out a system in which Lewis picked up clothing items—sometimes his choice, sometimes Crawley's—and held them up for inspection. Crawley showed a fondness for vivid colors.

"I'm not sure we should get such bright things." Lewis frowned at a pair of lime green yoga pants. "*These* would be less noticeable." He held up brown cords.

"Pah!" said Crawley. "Them breeches is the same as we've had all these years. No, lad, I wants a bit of color, and I'll wager the boys does, too."

Soon Lewis was struggling under a huge load that included Hawaiian shirts, fluorescent sports gear, tie-dyed T-shirts and an enormous pair of elastic-waisted, purple-flowered pants that must have belonged to a clown.

"For Bellows," explained Crawley. "And these"— a pair of gold satin basketball shorts rose from the pile—"are for me!"

The shorts dropped to the floor and then slowly began to rise and expand. Crawley was trying them on!

"No!" whispered Lewis, jerking at the shorts. "Not here." He glanced around. "There!"

A minute later, alone with Crawley in a changing room, Lewis piled the clothes onto a chair.

"Hurry," he said. "Please. I have to get home."

Crawley ignored him. Visible now, he was hauling on the shorts with an air of pride and satisfaction.

Lewis glanced away, into the mirror. He let out a gasp. The mirror didn't show Crawley at all! Only him, Lewis, staring at himself.

Noticing Lewis's consternation, Crawley grinned. "Looking glass don't work on the likes of us. But it's good to be in this secret room, lad, where I can see meself properly." He tugged at the shorts admiringly. "Now *these* are looking grand!"

"I . . . I'll wait outside." Lewis slipped out, then leaned against the door, catching his breath.

A sign caught his attention. "Costumes." What Crawley needed most, Lewis decided, was an eye patch.

He was poking through a bin of costume scraps—cowboy hats, magic wands, plastic Viking helmets—when he heard a voice.

"Hey! Lewis!"

He whirled around.

Abbie. She was wearing some kind of . . . hat? Pink wool. Red wool braids hanging down the sides. Pointy top. She looked so friendly, he almost glanced over his shoulder to see who she was *really* talking to.

"Uh . . . hey. Hello." Heat rose under his skin.

"Well, *this* is interesting. Did you follow me here? Or did I follow you?"

"Huh?"

She laughed. "Never mind. What do you think of this hat?" She twirled, holding up a braid.

He thought it made her look like an elf. The pointy top. Her wide mouth and too-big eyes. Would she *want* to look like an elf? He didn't answer.

She held out a poodle-shaped rhinestone pin. "How about this?"

Lewis struggled for words. "Very nice."

She laughed again, but not in a mean way. "What are *you* looking for?"

"I—um—gosh!" Suddenly, he remembered. Crawley!

He ran for the changing room and, without stopping to think, opened the door. There stood the pirate, resplendent in golden shorts and a red checked sports jacket, open to reveal a naked hairy torso. A thick ugly scar ran down his chest and disappeared into the shorts, emerging again above his left knee before vanishing into his boot. On his head was a neon orange baseball cap. "Tandy Bay Tigers," it said.

"Ain't I a picture?" Crawley threw out his arms and twirled, scraping his knuckles on the changing room walls.

Lewis froze in the doorway, aghast.

Crawley's good eye focused on something behind Lewis.

"Mam'selle," he said in an oily voice, with a surprisingly graceful bow.

"Oh . . ." said Abbie.

Lewis whirled. She was standing behind him, goggle-eyed.

"I'm . . ." she said, breathing hard. "I . . ."

It was the first time Lewis had seen her lost for words. His mind raced. "This is . . . my uncle Craw . . . Crawford."

"Your uncle?"

Lewis remembered the mirror. He threw out his arms to block her view.

"From Los Angeles," he blurted. The pirate had to be from *somewhere*. No one around here looked like that.

"Pleased to meet you, Mr. . . . Crawford," said Abbie. Lewis slammed the door.

Abbie continued to stand there, staring. "Whoa!" she said under her breath.

Lewis saw that he'd have to explain. "Los Angeles" provided an idea. "He's in the movies," said Lewis. "A stunt man."

"Oh," said Abbie, breathing a little easier. "So that's how he got . . ." She ran a hand down her body to indicate the long scar.

Lewis nodded.

"And the . . ." She pointed at her left eye.

Lewis nodded so hard, he felt dizzy.

"Wow! Must be dangerous work." Abbie peered again at the door.

"Yeah. Uh-huh. Dangerous." He waited for her to leave, but she just stood there, twirling her braid.

"I'd better help . . . you know." Lewis nodded toward the changing room.

"Oh. Okay. Is there anything special you're looking for?" She waved at the racks. "While I'm shopping?"

"No," said Lewis. "I mean, yes! A patch. An eye patch. For . . ." He jerked his head toward the changing room.

"Sure," she said. "Good idea. I'll keep an eye out . . . I mean . . ." She let out a giggle, then, to his surprise, colored red with embarrassment. "Sorry."

"That's okay," said Lewis.

She nodded. Then she smiled, wide. "Glad I got a chance to talk to you, Lewis. Finally!"

"Uh, yeah," said Lewis. "See you later."

"Later," she echoed, backing away. "Good-bye, Uncle Crawford!" she yelled at the changing room door.

Lewis watched her walk to the women's section. He waited a few minutes longer till she left the store. Then he slipped into the changing room.

"We have to go! Now!" he told the pirate, who was pulling on a pair of tight black cycling pants. Crawley opened his mouth.

"No arguments," said Lewis, surprising himself. "Now!"

"Aye, aye," said the captain. Lewis waited as the pirate faded into invisibility. Then he gathered up the clothing and walked, without stopping, to the cash register. He could tell the captain was with him by the pressure on his left arm.

"How much for all this?" he asked the cashier.

She stared at him suspiciously. He waited, breathing hard, while she added it up.

"$29.90," she said. Lewis paid and accepted two bulging shopping bags.

Outside, he studied the street nervously. People were driving home from work. The traffic was heavier.

He set off briskly, hoping that if they kept moving, Crawley wouldn't notice the cars. The bulky bags made it hard to walk, and he wished he could give one to Crawley. They were *his* clothes, after all.

They took the first quiet street. They hadn't gone far when Lewis came to a halt.

Two boys were shooting hoops in the driveway of a low blue bungalow. Both were dressed in white. Even at a distance, Lewis could pick out Seth.

He darted behind an elm tree, dragging Crawley with him.

"Hey!" yelled Seth. "It's Dearborn. Over there!"

Lewis heard the ball thump-thump to a stop. An instant later, the boys were in front of him. The second boy was Mike Burrows, also in his class.

Seth grinned. "What you got there, Lewisssser?" He reached into one of the bags.

Before Lewis could stop him, Seth whipped out the huge purple pants. "Hey, Burrows, check this out. Dearborn bought himself some cool—wow, I don't *believe* this! Hoo-eee!" Holding the pants by the waist and stretching them as wide as they would go, he started shrieking with laughter.

Mike joined him, pointing and doubling over.

"These aren't pants," yelled Seth. "This is a tent! Someone could *live* in these pants."

"A whole family!" howled Mike, grabbing one side of the pants and trying to stretch them further.

"Stop!" said Lewis, thinking of Bellows. "You're going to rip them."

That only made the boys laugh harder.

That's when Crawley stepped out from behind the tree. The boys froze as he bore down on them, his good eye flashing. Seizing them by the backs of their necks, Crawley hoisted them into the air.

"Drop them breeches, dogs!" he roared.

The pants fluttered to the ground. Lewis stuffed them into the bag.

Crawley, meanwhile, had turned Seth, floundering like a hooked fish, around to face him. The pirate's blind eye was up against Seth's face.

"I am going to cut out your liver, boy," he growled, in a voice like rolling thunder, "and I'm going to fasten it to the top of this tree! Does you think you'll look *pretty* without your liver?"

He gave Seth a shake.

"Nnn—" said Seth.

"A liver is one of them things you don't hardly think about. But I promise you, you'll miss it when it's gone!"

Crawley turned slowly from one captive to the other, breathing so heavily and with such rank fish breath that even Lewis could smell it. Both boys hung limp and terrified, unable to look away from the pirate's missing eye. Crawley shook them as easily as if they were kittens, making harsh, animal grunts.

Mike let out a sob.

"Pah!" said the pirate and dropped them both.

They crumpled in a heap and lay there, stunned, before scrambling to their feet. Lewis watched as they ran shakily toward the house.

"And now, laddie" came a weary voice behind him, "might we go home?"

16

Streetlights blinked on as Lewis and his invisible companion walked home. Cars honked and whooshed past, but Lewis noticed none of it, still stunned by the incredible sight of Crawley shaking Seth—like a terrier shaking a rat!

"I never liked the cat o' nine tails," announced the voice to his left. "Felt the pain of the whip meself in my younger days. But, by thunder, if anyone deserves its sting, it's them two sharks. I'd give 'em thirty lashes each, if they was on my ship!"

Lewis shook his head. "That's not how we do things these days."

"Oh?" said the pirate. "And how *does* you do things,

139

lad, if you doesn't mind me asking? When you comes up against a pair of bottom-feeders like them, how does you take the wind out of their sails?"

"We . . ." The truth was, Lewis didn't know. If he knew, he wouldn't have been plagued by Seth all this time.

"There's a lot to be said for cutting out a liver," grumbled Crawley. "Slows a body down."

"No," said Lewis. "Cutting out a liver is . . . is *inappropriate!*" Putting down his shopping bags, he glared at the space to his left.

And then, out of nowhere, he started to laugh. It bubbled up like a geyser, impossible to stop. Suddenly, it all seemed ridiculous. Crawley. The pirates. Even Seth. Mostly, Lewis laughed at himself. *Inappropriate? Where had that come from?*

The shopping bags, which had been resting beside his feet, began floating down the street.

"Stop!" yelled Lewis, a new bubble of hilarity rising as he raced after the bags. "Put them down!"

Aside from the laughing, which he attributed to some kind of hysteria (he wasn't *used* to laughing), he reached home without further incident. He still had to sneak into Shornoway, of course, which was no small matter with two overstuffed shopping bags and an invisible pirate dragging from his arm. Tiptoeing past the kitchen, he heard the chirruping sound of Mrs. Binchy's chatter, followed by his father's rumble. Garlicky smells filled the hall.

Upstairs, the pirates made no attempt to conceal their joy at seeing Crawley again. They clutched at their captain with a kind of desperate relief, as if they hadn't expected him to return. Lewis, carrying the bags, was treated like a hero, too. Soon the clothing was flying out, looking like giant, swooping butterflies as the pirates swirled it above their heads.

Watching them, Lewis smiled.

"Aye, lad," said Crawley. "We done it, didn't we? We brought back the treasure."

Treasure? Lewis would never have imagined that secondhand clothes could be described that way. But looking around, he saw that it was true.

"Did you ever see anything so grand?" asked Adam, holding a pair of red jeans against his body.

"Not since them rubies we took off the *Barbary Ellen*, there in the Indian Ocean. You look a prince," said Moyle, "and see what a gent I looks in this!" He wore an apple-green cowboy shirt with gold fringe— one of Crawley's choices. It was several sizes too small and the spaces between the buttons gaped open, revealing a pale, blue-veined chest.

But the happiest pirate of all was Jonas. Knowing how chilly he got, Lewis had put aside a fleecy pink tracksuit just for him. Jonas crooned with delight as he pulled it on. "So warm," he said, stroking the fabric. "Like the finest of furs. I ain't been this cozy since we left the southern seas."

Soon there was a kind of bizarre fashion show going on, with the pirates cheering and clapping as one, then another, paraded his new finery. They couldn't have been more pleased or proud.

Not so, Lewis. The longer he watched, the more his heart sank. The smile on his face became more and more forced.

It wasn't going to work.

The pirates did *not* look like tourists. Not even remotely. He was the only one in the room with any sense of modern clothing, so he was the only one who could see the truth. They looked like clowns! And not even ordinary clowns. With their scars and beards and long greasy pigtails, they looked like clowns who had joined the Hell's Angels. *Biker* clowns! To someone meeting them on the street, they'd be scarier than ever.

He couldn't possibly take them to the museum looking like this. He remembered Abbie's shock when she first saw Crawley in the changing room. How would she react to *seven* Crawleys?

Lewis would have to tell them.

But not yet. Not while they were having so much fun.

He sank heavily onto his bed. He couldn't think anymore, not with all this craziness. To his right was Barnaby Bellows's huge stomach—bouncing and jiggling, stretching the flowered pants to their limit. Higher up was a yellow sweatshirt Bellows had fashioned into a bonnet, the sleeves tied under his chin.

He looks like he's going to a Halloween party, thought Lewis.

The thought took a moment to root. He sucked in his breath sharply.

"Halloween," he whispered.

Jumping to his feet, he waved his arms. "Halloween!" he yelled. *"Halloween!"*

The pirates paused in their antics.

"I've got it!" he told them. "We have to *wait* to go the museum—till October 31st. Halloween!"

Crawley stepped forward. He was wearing gold basketball shorts, black boots and nothing else. "I sees no reason—"

"It's perfect," interrupted Lewis. "On Halloween, Tandy Bay is full of . . . unusual-looking people. Everyone's dressed up. Everyone looks . . . er, different. You'll fit right in!"

"Halloween?" said Adam. "Does you mean All Hallows Eve? When ghosts walk abroad?"

"*We* used to walk abroad on All Hallows Eve," said Jonas, "but when folks started racing in them things that goes so fast—"

"That's another advantage of Halloween!" said Lewis. "People drive their cars slowly, because of all the kids who are out."

A smile dawned on Jonas's face. "If the children can face them cars," he said, "I suppose we can, too."

Crawley snorted. "Them cars ain't so terrible. I faced 'em today, didn't I? I weren't afeared a bit."

The pirates nodded, impressed.

Halloween could actually work, thought Lewis, feeling his first real confidence in the plan. The pirates would just have to wait, that's all.

The kitchen bell rang, and he had to go down to dinner. When he returned, the pirates demanded their usual evening reading. It was a long chapter, and Lewis was so tired he fell asleep in the middle of a sentence.

It wasn't until breakfast the next day that he remembered the *disadvantages* of waiting for Halloween. Actually, there was only one.

Timing.

If the pirates waited till Halloween, they would still be at Shornoway for the class visit.

He let out a groan.

"Lewis?" said his mother. "Are you all right? Do you feel okay?"

Lewis dodged the motherly hand that was closing in on his forehead. "I'm fine!" he yelled. "I have to go."

He rushed out of the kitchen so quickly he knocked over a chair, but not fast enough to miss his mother's remark: "It must be puberty."

Lewis turned to face her. "It is *not!*" he yelled back. "This is *not* puberty!"

With so many things on his mind, it was perhaps not surprising that he got all the way to school before he remembered . . .

Seth.

Who had been shaken like a rat the night before.

Who probably hadn't forgotten.

17

Lewis saw the white pants coming his way as he walked into school. Dirt-gray at the bottoms. Frayed. The blue-and-white shoes.

He lunged into a crowd of kids.

A quick movement to his left. A girl's squeal. Something—an elbow? a fist?—rammed him in the ribs, hard. He caved at the waist, gasping, as Seth ran past.

The pain was dull. But each time he inhaled, it got sharper.

He sat very still through the morning, taking light, shallow breaths. In the playground, he stayed close to Mrs. Reber, not caring if he looked babyish.

But then a little kid fell down, and Mrs. Reber had to help. It gave Seth another chance.

He crept up as lightly as a panther. "So where's your big goon, Lewisser? Your babysitter?"

Forming his fingers into a gun, Seth aimed it straight at Lewis. He made a small explosive sound. Pow!

"Who's gonna help you *here*, Dearborn?"

Lewis stared at the ground.

Later, walking home, he watched warily for an ambush. Hedges, fences, lanes. His rib cage ached.

Mrs. Dearborn's car was in the drive. She was home early. There was another car there, too—a silver one he didn't recognize.

"Is someone here?" he asked Mrs. Binchy. She was polishing the old clock in the front hall, something he'd never seen her do before. There was a stormy look on her face.

"Real estate agents," she muttered. "Your mother's showing them around."

"What?" said Lewis. "She said they weren't coming till Friday."

"She changed it. They've been crawling over the house all afternoon. Jackals on a carcass. It's not right."

Lewis nodded. Mrs. Binchy never hesitated to speak up. The whole family knew her feelings about Shornoway.

147

"Where are they now? The agents?" he asked.

She sniffed. "They've finished the Grand Tour. They're in *there*." She nodded toward the parlor.

There were two of them. The man was lanky and stoop-shouldered, with a grin that revealed large, even teeth. He shook Lewis's hand, heartily but kiddingly as if Lewis were four years old. The woman barely glanced at Lewis, which was okay with him. He didn't like her lipstick. Red and sticky-looking.

They were standing at the parlor window. Lewis's mother stood beside them, looking uncomfortable, as she always did with company.

"The house inspection is mostly a formality," said the woman. "Of course, we're not positive these clients will come through, but it looks extremely promising, and as I say, they're planning all new construction."

"Ground up," added the man. "Three levels—gift shop, pizza parlor, karaoke bar. Maybe even a small casino."

"Excuse me?" said Lewis.

"They've been waiting years for the right property to come along." The man chuckled. "Years! Hard to find a big chunk of waterfront land these days. And a view like this? Amazing! The pool could go right where we're standing and—"

"*Excuse me?*" said Lewis again. Having had practice in interrupting the pirates, he put enough force behind it this time to make the man stop. All three adults stared.

"Lewis?" said his mother.

"What . . . what's going on? What does he mean, a pool? We're in a *room*."

The man smiled. "Sure, but imagine all this gone, and a great big swimming pool here instead, with a slide and a deep end and—"

"I *know* what a swimming pool looks like."

"Lewis!" His mother glared.

"Hot tub," added the man. "You could probably get visiting privileges in the contract. Come here any time you want. Sauna, small gym—"

"But what's going to happen to the parlor?" persisted Lewis, pointing at the shabby walls. This room was right below Libertalia.

"Lewis, you're being rude," said his mother. "Mr. Winnaker's talking about a *new* building. A resort. I'll explain later. Don't you have homework?"

Suddenly, Lewis got it. "They're going to tear down Shornoway?" His voice grew shrill, soaring into the squeaky notes he hated.

"All right, that's enough. Go to your room, Lewis."

He glared at his mother, but she stared back even more fiercely, her jaw set. Lewis stumbled into the hall.

Mrs. Binchy was listening at the door. "A crying shame," she muttered, as Lewis dashed past.

He looked for his father in the kitchen, then ran to the study.

"Hey! You're home." Mr. Dearborn closed the book he'd been reading. "Dinner will—"

"Never mind that." Lewis's voice still squeaked, but he didn't care. "Do you *know* what they're doing?"

"Who?"

"Those real estate people. They're going to tear down Shornoway. Put up some resort place with a karaoke bar."

For a long time, his dad just stared. Then he folded his hands on his desk. "Oh."

"Gift shop, too," said Lewis, although he wasn't sure what difference that made.

"Gift shop," repeated his dad. "Ah."

Was it *ah* or *aw*? Mr. Dearborn's pouchy face had gone even droopier than usual. Lewis was pretty sure it was *aw*.

He sat down across from his father, who had taken off his glasses to rub his eyes.

"Make them stop," said Lewis. "Please?"

"Lewis, I—"

"Why can't we just *stay* here?" It was the first time he'd said it. Even to himself.

His father gave him the saddest smile he'd ever seen. "Lewis, I can't. It's your mother's inheritance.

Her choice. And you *know* the first thing she'd say: how can we afford to keep this place up? I wish . . ." He shrugged helplessly.

Lewis nodded. He understood.

As he struggled to take it in—Shornoway razed to the ground, replaced by a fancy resort—Mrs. Binchy's voice sang out from the hall. "Lewis? You have a guest, dear."

Lewis exchanged confused glances with his father. Then he turned to the doorway.

Abbie!

She was standing there with Mrs. Binchy. In one hand, she held a white plastic bag. In the other was a leash that led to a small wire-haired dog at her feet. Black eyes stared back at Lewis.

"I hope it's okay." Abbie glanced past Lewis at Mr. Dearborn. "I found something for you, Lewis, and I had to walk Winston anyhow, so . . ."

Lewis didn't answer. Couldn't.

Finally, Mrs. Binchy jumped in. "Of course it's okay. What a dear girl! This is young Abbie," she told Mr. Dearborn. "From Lewis's class at school."

Mr. Dearborn looked as amazed as Lewis to see a girl and a dog in his study.

Abbie reached into the bag. "I found this at the drugstore. I know you wanted a secondhand one, but it didn't cost much new." She held out a piece of black cloth with elastic attached.

Lewis stared, transfixed.

"It's an eye patch." Pulling the elastic over her head, she settled the patch across one eye. "See? For your Uncle Crawford."

All eyes focused on the patch. Mr. Dearborn frowned in an effort to understand. Mrs. Binchy adjusted her glasses to get a better look. Then she put her hands on her hips. "Uncle Crawford! Now who might *he* be, if you don't mind me asking?"

It was like sinking into quicksand, thought Lewis.

"No one," he bleated. "Nothing."

Before Abbie could get him in deeper, he grabbed her arm and pulled her down the hall, heading for the front door. Winston toddled behind.

Suddenly, voices approached—his mother and the real estate people. Lewis glanced at Abbie, still wearing the eye patch. Panic seized him. He made a sharp turn toward the back staircase, towing his little train behind.

"Lewis! What are you doing?" Abbie forced him to a halt.

"Come see my room? Please?" It was the only thing he could think of.

Moments later, when they were actually there— standing outside Libertalia—he panicked again.

"Never mind. Bad idea. Let's go back down."

"For Pete's sake, Lewis! Do you have any idea how weird you're being?" Abbie turned the knob sharply and stepped into Libertalia.

He closed his eyes. A long silence followed. So long he grew anxious. He burst through the doorway.

She was standing in the middle of Libertalia, holding Winston and the eye patch. Stroking the dog's head, she gazed around at the eight tall walls. "This is some room you've got here, Lewis Dearborn. It's making my skin tingle."

"The wind," said Lewis. "I'll close—"

"No, leave it. It's not the wind. Something else. I'm trying to figure it out."

Lewis nodded nervously.

She put Winston down and began a slow tour of the room. Picking up the bottle, she peeked at the tiny sailor. "How did they get the ship inside? Do you know?"

He shook his head.

Behind them, Winston let out a warning growl.

They turned. The dog was in front of the red door. His gray fur bristled, and his mouth was pulled back in a snarl.

"Heeeey, Winston," said Abbie. "What's the matter?"

The growl rose to a whine. Then a piercing yip.

"Come here, puppy!" Abbie crouched and held out her arms. "There's nothing there."

Winston ignored her. Barking fiercely, he scratched at the bottom of the door. He turned to Abbie with sharp angry yelps as if to demand, "Open up!"

"What's behind there?" Abbie hesitated, then reached for the knob and turned.

Lewis waited, his heart pounding. The door seemed to be stuck shut. Unless . . . it was *held* shut?

Abbie glanced back at her dog. He was growling again, his whole body trembling as he stared at the door.

"Wow!" said Abbie. "I've never seen him do this. It's like he's seeing a ghost."

Lewis held his breath. Silent.

"Hey, that's funny! Did you know there are stories about this house? My grandma said, when she was a girl, they used to think it was—" She stopped.

Lewis *knew* he should make some light, kidding remark. He should say, "Ha-ha. Good joke." But his voice would betray him, he knew it would. All he could do was blink.

He was blinking too quickly, he realized. He was turning red, too.

"Lewis?" Abbie peered at his face, alarmed. Then, "You're *not* serious!"

Lewis still couldn't speak.

"Is it true? Your house is haunted?"

He looked away.

"I thought . . ." said Abbie breathlessly. "Everybody thinks it's just . . . oh, Lewis."

"Let's go," he begged suddenly, staring into her eyes and willing himself to stop blinking. "Please?"

She stood frozen a moment longer, then snatched up the still-growling Winston. They walked down the upstairs hall without a word. But at the top of the staircase, Lewis grabbed Abbie's arm again.

"Don't talk about Uncle Crawford, okay?"

Her eyes grew huge. "Uncle Crawford is the . . .?"

Lewis thought about denying it, or at least shaking his head. But in the strength of her direct gaze, he was helpless. She was reading his thoughts so clearly, they might as well have been billboards.

He nodded.

"Okay," she said. "Okay."

Up the stairs came a warbling voice. "Yoo-hoo. Would you kids like a snack?"

"Coming!" yelled Lewis.

He turned to ask—

"I won't say a word," said Abbie.

He had to trust her.

He had no choice.

18

Lewis's legs felt wobbly as he climbed the stairs to Libertalia that night. The pirates must have heard his whole conversation with Abbie. They must have heard him tell her that Shornoway was haunted. Would they be angry?

They turned out to be much more interested in the dog.

"Best to keep dogs out of here, lad," said Moyle, nodding sagely. "Dogs can feel things what humans miss."

"Can't keep no secret from a dog," agreed Jonas.

"Nor from a rat!" added Jack, sniffing at Lewis's clothing.

What upset them much more was the news about Shornoway.

"Nawww!" groaned Crawley, rearing back in disbelief. "We saw them reely-statey people with our own eyes today when they pranced theirselves through this tower. We didn't like a hair of them, lad, not a hair! And now they're going to tear down Shornoway? A lovely manse like this? Why, it's practically new!"

Adam nodded. "I remembers like yesterday when they put in the windows. All these high ones here, and them others downstairs with the stained and leaded glass. Pretty as a cathedral! It were the grandest house on the whole coast."

"Still is," said Bellows loyally. "There ain't no call to tear it down. Better we tears off the heads of those reely-statey people. That's what *I* thinks!"

"Aye," growled Jack. "Tear off their heads!"

"Aye! Aye!" cried the others.

Lewis couldn't help being sympathetic, but he felt obliged to step in. "There will be no tearing off of heads. This is the twenty-first century. We don't *do* that."

"We don't *do* that," imitated Jack in a high, mincy voice.

Hoping to distract them, Lewis opened *Treasure Island*. Within minutes, they were transported to distant Southern Seas. The ship had reached the island now, with its thundering surf and its windless, sweltering heat. Reading Robert Louis Stevenson's words, Lewis was as captivated as the pirates.

But the longer he read, the more he wished it were *him* on that island. Jim Hawkins had problems, true, but bad as they were, they didn't seem nearly as complicated as his own. And now he had Abbie to worry about, too—a girl whose main talent was talking! Would she keep his secret?

And would he have to talk to her now at school?

He didn't. The moment Lewis stepped through the doors of Tandy Bay Elementary, shyness enveloped him like an old familiar cloak. His habit of ducking people was so strong that even if Abbie had wanted to talk to him, she wouldn't have had a chance.

Lewis watched her, though, especially when she was with friends. Was she telling? If so, surely they'd be staring at him—a boy who had *ghosts* in his house. But his classmates continued to ignore him.

For the next week, heavy rain kept Tandy Bay students inside. Lewis hid in the library during breaks. He discovered some new books about pirates in the non-fiction section. One even had a page about Libertalia.

The rain also saved him from Seth, who came into the library only when he had to. Still, Lewis couldn't avoid him entirely. One morning, when Ms. Forsley's back was turned, Seth stuck his foot into the aisle as Lewis passed, sending Lewis crashing onto a small, awkward girl named Charlene. Lewis grabbed Charlene's shoulder to steady himself, and his face nearly touched hers. The other kids laughed—it must have looked like kissing. Charlene looked ready to cry.

Abbie passed back a note. *Why do you let him?*

Lewis bristled. What did she know, anyway? He was actually getting off *easily* with Seth these days.

The library was like a cocoon. He hoped the stormy weather would last. As long as it rained, he could let himself relax—which he did, with the result that he was completely unprepared for what happened next.

It was early on a Friday morning. Announcements droned through the classroom speaker. Abbie gazed out the window. Lewis, bored, wondered about the painted sticks that held her hair in a knot at the back of her head. Were they chopsticks?

Suddenly, Abbie stiffened. Her eyes opened wide.

Lewis followed her gaze to the window. At first, he didn't see anything. Then, in the lower right corner, he spotted a flash of neon orange.

A shiver ran through him. He *knew* that color. Crawley's new baseball cap!

No, he thought, closing his eyes. Hearing a gasp behind him, he looked again, in time to see the captain's ravaged face appear in the classroom window, the peak on his cap dripping with rain. Seeing that he'd caught Lewis's attention, Crawley winked— which, in his case, meant closing his only working eye. The missing eye was now covered by his new eye patch, which he had adopted with great pleasure after Abbie's visit.

Someone near Lewis laughed nervously.

Ms. Forsley glanced up from her attendance book. "Abbie? Is there a problem?"

Abbie shook her head. Ms. Forsley returned to her task.

Glancing out again, Lewis froze in horror. Standing beside Crawley, looking frightened, was Barnaby Bellows. He was drenched to the skin in an undersized yellow sweatshirt, and he clung to the captain's arm as he squinted through the window. Both pirates were searching for—Lewis suddenly understood— him! Crawley was pointing and speaking. Lewis couldn't hear the words, but he could guess. *Lookee there, Bellows. There's the lad at his schoolwork. Ain't he a sight?*

The room filled with whispers and titters as more kids spotted the strangers. Bellows's size alone was enough to draw gasps, not to mention his skin color. Fear had given his skin an eerie, greenish glow.

"What's going on?" Ms. Forsley glanced around, then turned to the window.

Gone.

No, thought Lewis, overwhelmed by a feeling of doom. Not gone.

Still out there.

Hiding. Waiting.

He held up his hand.

Ms. Forsley frowned. "Yes, Lewis?"

"May I please go to the washroom?"

She nodded.

He forced himself to *walk* to the classroom door. There was a splutter, then a squawk, from the speaker, and the announcements died. Once in the hall, Lewis broke into a run, slowing only when he reached the office. Some kind of commotion was going on inside. He quick-walked past and crashed through the heavy front door. Outside, he bent into a crouch to stay below the windows as he hurried along the front wall. Rain pelted his back and head. Rounding the corner, he saw the pirates—still peeking into his classroom, their backs turned.

They must have *followed* him to school. How many classrooms had they peeked into first? Were they the cause of the fuss in the office? He scrambled along the wall, staying low.

When he tapped Bellows's arm, the pirate let out a yell that could have been heard in Shornoway. "GARRRRRR!"

"Shhhh!" hissed Lewis, waving both hands. "Be quiet! Captain Crawley, what are you *doing* here?"

Crawley joined Lewis in a crouch.

"Welllll," he drawled, not the slightest bit concerned, "the boys was getting a mite nervy about leaving, so I thought it best to give them—just one at a time, like—a bit of practice. So as not to be such a shock when we leaves for good."

"Shock?" cried Lewis. "Shock? What do you call this?" He waved at his classroom window. Then he glanced over his shoulder, wondering how long it would take for the principal to show up, followed by a posse of teachers.

"Don't get yourself in a stir, lad. We're just testing the waters, so to speak. Trying out these new garments. It's a grand thing for Bellows here and—"

"Bellows?" said Lewis incredulously. "This isn't for Bellows! This is for *you*, Captain Crawley, because you're bored with staying home. You're starting to *enjoy* being out in the world, aren't you, now that you're not so scared anymore? Bellows? Look at him. He's a wet noodle!"

Barnaby Bellows, who had indeed been looking wilted and noodle-ish, drew himself up to his full eight feet. "Noodle?" he said.

Lewis was aware, in his peripheral vision, of faces in the window.

"Get down," he begged Bellows. "Please! You shouldn't be here. Go home!"

A cloud of stubbornness came over Crawley's face. He rose and planted his feet firmly in the gravel. Beside him, Bellows crossed arms thick as tree trunks over his chest.

Ms. Forsley was in the window frame now. She was beckoning.

"Go!" Lewis told the pirates. "Now! Or . . ." He searched frantically for a threat. "Or I'll stop reading *Treasure Island*. You'll never know the ending. Ever!"

Their faces crumpled.

"Nah!" said Bellows, in disbelief.

Giddy with power, Lewis rose to *his* full height. "Go! I mean it. Now!"

The pirates lingered, uncertain. Then slowly they retreated across the playground, whispering and bumping into one another.

Lewis forced himself to look at his classroom window. They were standing there, watching. Everybody. His whole class.

He sighed heavily. Then he trudged back to the front door, shivering in his wet clothes. Mrs. Chan, the principal, was in her office, looking agitated. When she spotted Lewis, she called out. He broke into a run. Reaching his classroom, he burst through the door and slid neatly into his desk.

The only sound was his heart beating.

"Lewis?" Ms. Forsley's voice was a few notes higher than normal. "May I speak to you, please?"

Legs shaky, he walked to her desk.

"Carry on with your work," she told the class. Of course, no one so much as shuffled a paper.

"Lewis, Abbie says that man . . . one of those men . . . is your uncle. Visiting from Los Angeles?"

Lewis glanced at Abbie. He swallowed hard. "Uh, yes."

"Well, I don't know how they do things in Los Angeles, but here in Tandy Bay Elementary, we have rules about school visitors. If your uncle wants to talk to you, Lewis, if there's some emergency—"

"No emergency," Lewis whispered, but with the room so silent, he knew they could all hear. "He just didn't understand."

"I see," said Ms. Forsley. "But, of course, *you* understand, Lewis, that you're not supposed to leave the building without permission."

"I know. I'm sorry. It won't happen again. He—my uncle—he gets it now."

"I see," said Ms. Forsley again, although it was clear she didn't see at all. Her face was very pink. If it got any pinker, it would look like *his*. "Take your seat, Lewis."

At that moment, Mrs. Chan popped her head through the door. She was panting, and it took her a moment to speak. "Everything all right here?"

Ms. Forsley cleared her throat. "Fine. I'll explain later."

Lewis slumped low in his seat, wishing he had the pirates' gift of invisibility. As Ms. Forsley drew a diagram on the board, he had an itchy feeling, as if dozens of eyes were boring into the back of his head.

He turned.

Dozens of eyes *were* boring. The most obvious were Seth's. His eyes were bugging out, the whites showing prominently.

Lewis turned away in a panic. But the thought that followed was simple and clear.

How could the other kids *not* stare? After what had just happened? He'd been arguing with two ghosts from the eighteenth century in full view of his entire class. What did he expect?

He took a deep breath. Then another. Catching his eye, Ms. Forsley asked him a question about the problem on the board. It was a yes-or-no question.

Lewis felt the familiar heat race through his body. He felt the red in his skin.

"Yes," he said after a moment. His voice squeaked, but only a little. No one laughed.

He sat up straight. Took another breath.

The hot feeling eased.

19

"**T**wo?" said Abbie, breathlessly. "There are *two* ghosts?"

He had ducked out of school quickly, but she'd caught up a block away. She must have run.

He thought about saying yes, two. Then he thought— two, three, four, what was the difference?

"Seven," he said. "Altogether."

"Seven!" It was enough to make her sway on the sidewalk. "There are *seven* ghosts in your house?"

"Actually, they're in my room." The words tumbled out in a rush. "They live there." Lewis was surprised how good it felt to say it out loud. Exhilarating, even. He had kept the pirates' secret for so long. Talking about them was like releasing a held-back sneeze.

"They *live* there?" repeated Abbie. "You mean . . . like roommates?"

"Well," said Lewis, "yes. Sort of."

"But aren't they . . . dead?"

"I know," he said. "It's not like you expect."

"They seem almost—"

"Yes," said Lewis. "Exactly!"

"And you're not—"

"Oh, no. I was in the beginning. But then I got used to having them around, and now they don't scare me at all. Except maybe Jack the Rat. I guess *he'd* scare anyone. And one of them is just our age. Adam."

"Adam," repeated Abbie. "How . . . how did he die?"

"The same way they all died. Drowned at sea."

"Oh." She nodded as if this were finally something she understood. "Fishermen."

Good guess, thought Lewis. Tandy Bay had a long history of fishermen lost at sea.

He shook his head no. Now that he'd begun, it seemed impossible to hold back. "They're pirates."

Her eyes widened. "Pirates?"

He nodded.

She searched his face, looking for signs of a joke. "You mean it, don't you?"

He nodded again.

She let out a groan. "Lewis Dearborn, *you* are something! You sit there every day like . . . well, I'm sorry, but you're probably the wimpiest kid on the planet. Meanwhile, when you go home, in your *room* . . ." She shook her head, unable to finish.

"I know. It's weird."

"This is beyond weird, Lewis. What do these ghosts of yours do? I mean, do they moan? Rattle chains? Do they—hey, you know what? I don't even know what *questions* to ask!"

So Lewis explained. He told her how it had begun, with Great-Granddad and Libertalia. Then he described how he'd met Crawley and the others. As he talked, they began to walk. The closer they got to his house, the more the wind picked up, and the more they had to huddle together so she could hear. When he told her about reading to the pirates, she smiled.

"Geez. Sounds like storytime at the library."

"Yes!" he said, excited that she'd seen it, too. "That's how I felt at first. But later, I started to really like the book myself. *Treasure Island.*"

"Never read it," she said.

"It's good. Old. But exciting."

She smiled again. He was surprised at how warm he felt, even with the wind howling through his jacket. It felt *good* to talk to a live human being his own age.

But as they approached Shornoway, the old nervousness returned. Would he have to invite her in?

She must have noticed. "I'd better go. Maybe I'll stop at the library on the way home. Pick up a copy of that book. *Treasure Island.*"

He nodded and walked away.

She called after him. "Hey, Lewis?"

"Yeah?"

"Thanks. For the pirate story." She waved and broke into an awkward run.

Which pirate story, wondered Lewis. Then he smiled, realizing she had meant for him to wonder.

Up in Libertalia, the pirates were nowhere in sight. They were around, though. He could tell by the fishy smell. Hiding, thought Lewis. Because of Crawley's stunt outside the school.

Dinner that night was duck in cherry sauce, mashed potatoes and something called roasted Jerusalem artichokes. It was served with lavish explanations by Mr. Dearborn.

"The food is excellent, Gerald," said Mrs. Dearborn as her husband sat down, "but look at you! You're still wearing your cooking apron! It has cherry stains all over it."

"Oh!" said her husband, whipping it off. "Yes, yes, of course. Sorry."

"Honestly, you're beginning to look like my students. They dress as if they're going to the beach—or to bed. One of the girls wears *pajamas* to class."

"Sorry," said Mr. Dearborn again. "But, you know, that reminds me of something. I saw the oddest fellow today, out the window. Some kind of tramp, I suppose. He was roaming around the yard. If you think your students dress oddly, Charlotte, you should have seen *this* fellow."

Lewis, who was about to eat a forkful of duck, lowered it to his plate. "What . . . what did he look like?"

Mr. Dearborn frowned. "Thin and hunched over. Pale as a mushroom. Poor soul looked as though he'd been living in a cellar. But the strangest thing was his clothes. Baggy striped pants and a frilly . . . well, I suppose it was a lady's blouse. To top it all off, he was barefoot. In this weather!"

Jack the Rat, thought Lewis miserably. His favorite outfit.

"I went out to see what he wanted. I thought he might be lost or ill."

"That was good of you," said Mrs. Dearborn. Then, "Close your mouth, Lewis. I can see your tonsils."

"Sorry," said Lewis.

"By the time I got outside," Mr. Dearborn continued, "he was gone. Must have run off. Very odd."

Lewis let out a slow sigh. It was worse than he thought. The pirates had made at least *two* excursions out of Shornoway.

"Well, never mind." Mr. Dearborn shrugged. "Let's talk about something more cheerful—like next Tuesday. Your class visit, Lewis! Mrs. Binchy and I have a few surprises."

"What do you mean?" If there was one thing Lewis did *not* need, it was more surprises.

"You'll see," said his father mysteriously.

"Dad, please!"

"Okay, I'll give you a hint. There'll be some food surprises. Well, you probably guessed that. But I'm also going to make a little speech."

"What?" squawked Lewis. "Dad, you can't make *speeches* on a school visit!"

"Now, Lewis, I've already spoken to Ms. Forsley, and she thought it was an excellent idea. Don't worry, it won't take long. I'm sure your classmates will enjoy it."

"I imagine they might *learn* something, too," added Mrs. Dearborn dryly.

Lewis stifled a groan. Was there any possible speech his father could make that his classmates would enjoy? He racked his brain. None.

And was there any way he could *stop* his father,

without hurting his feelings? Lewis racked his brain again. Same answer.

His feet felt like lead weights as he climbed to Libertalia that night. Things were getting out of control. He couldn't stop his father, he couldn't stop the real estate agents . . .

But maybe he could still stop the pirates. He *had* to put an end to their excursions.

He opened the door to see Crawley miming a tiptoeing walk. The other pirates were laughing. Lewis could tell what was going on—the captain was acting out his visit to Tandy Bay School.

"For Pete's sake!" he said. "Listen, Captain Crawley, if you want to get back to your ship, you're going to have to start to behave yourself."

"Beeeeehaaaaave meself?" Crawley shouted with laughter, and the others joined in. "Laddie, I'm a pirate! A robber. A blackguard. A thief."

"Beeeeeeehaaaaaaave!" chortled Moyle. "Now there's a good jest, ain't it?"

"Beeeehaaaave," repeated the others, mincing about like courtiers dancing a minuet.

"We're the scurviest villains who ever walked a deck," shouted Crawley. "The scourge of the seven seas!"

Before the others could take up the chorus, Lewis interrupted. "I don't believe you."

The room went instantly quiet.

"Pardon?" said Adam.

"I don't believe you were that bad," said Lewis. "I mean, you *say* lots of awful things." He remembered the liver-cutting threat. "But I don't believe you *did* that many terrible things. I just don't believe it."

The pirates glanced at one another. For a moment, Lewis thought they were going to agree. And then, with a horrific "ARRGGGH!" Crawley whipped out his sword. With lightning speed, he slashed the chilly air, just inches from Lewis's nose. Lewis could *feel* the breeze as the blade sliced past. A second later, the whole crew was running amok, yelling foul words and waving their cutlasses.

"Okay!" cried Lewis, raising his hands in surrender. "Okay! You're scurvy. You're bad!"

Smiling sweetly, Crawley sheathed his sword. "Just so long as you knows."

"Aye!" shouted Jack. Reluctant to put away *his* dagger, he swished it back and forth in rapid figure eights, the metal glinting in the lamplight. He was wearing the ruffled blouse and striped pants Mr. Dearborn had described.

Lewis reached for *Treasure Island*. He held the book in front of him like a shield.

"Before I read," he said slowly and carefully, "we

have to talk about these little 'practice' trips you're taking. Outside. Wearing your tourist clothes. You can't do that anymore."

"Can't?" snarled Jack, darting forward.

"Shouldn't," corrected Lewis. "If you want me to help, you'll have to trust me. No more going outside. And when my class comes to visit next week, *please* stay invisible."

Jack froze. They all did.

"Class?" squeaked Skittles. "More strangers?"

Uh-oh, thought Lewis. He'd forgotten to tell them.

Deal with it, he told himself.

Quickly, clearly, he explained the class visit. The more timid of the pirates continued to look anxious. Skittles glowed like a flashlight.

"Don't worry," said Lewis as soothingly as he could. "The people in my class are kids. That's not really the same as *strangers*, is it? And they'll only be here a short time. It might even be good for you, a chance to see how regular people look and act. You could . . . you could watch and learn!"

He was making it up as he went along. The logic sounded feeble, even to him. He was surprised when the pirates bought it.

"The lad says true," said Moyle. "Here's a chance to learn the ropes."

Crawley perked up, too. "A chance to get ourselves more practice. I likes this plan. We puts on our new garments, like, and joins in the class. They won't even notice us!"

"Aye!" yelled a few bold souls.

"NO!" cried Lewis, louder than he intended. "No dressing up! No joining in! Just *watching*! Please, please, stay invisible while they're here."

He started to explain why this was important, but the pirates had lost interest.

"Long John!" they shouted. "Give us Long John Silver!"

Lewis sighed and opened *Treasure Island*. For the next hour, he forgot his problems. For the next hour, he was far away on a mysterious tropical island. For the next hour, he didn't have to worry about a thing.

20

On the day of the class visit, Lewis woke before dawn. He squinted at the glowing numbers on his bedside clock. 5:04 a.m.

Closing his eyes, he tried not to imagine all the things that could go wrong with this day. His mother, for example, telling everyone how he'd learned to read while still in diapers. Mrs. Binchy grabbing kids' wrists and calling them skinny-minnies. His father making some kind of . . . *speech*!

As for the pirates? Might as well try to control a storm at sea.

———

For Lewis, the strangeness started with the peculiar experience of going on a field trip to his own house. The class, including him, arrived mid-morning. As Ms. Forsley led her students up the driveway, she talked about Shornoway as if it were a museum, pointing out the gables, the wrought iron and the stained-glass windows. She didn't seem to mind that some of the windows were cracked or boarded over. She just said it was a shame, and wouldn't it be wonderful if they could be restored?

When the door opened, it was Mrs. Binchy who rushed out to greet them. She looked just as Lewis had expected, dead-Fred slippers and all. Her dress, as always, was a saggy old thing. Beneath it, her old-lady bosom swayed, like a couple of animals trapped in a bag.

The surprise was that she knew some of the kids.

"Ryan, dearie, how's your grandma? She wasn't at choir practice last week. Is the cold worse?"

"She's better now, thank you, Mrs. Binchy," said Ryan.

"And Sophie Duval, is that you? Why, the last time I saw you, you were riding that little pink training-wheels bike."

Sophie colored slightly, but smiled back. "I have a full-sized bike now, Mrs. Binchy."

178

Well, of course, thought Lewis to himself. Of course, Mrs. Binchy would know other people. She had lived in Tandy Bay all her life, and it wasn't a big place. For some reason, Lewis had never thought of her having a life outside of Shornoway, with people and activities that didn't concern him.

She shooed the class into the front hallway now, where Mr. and Mrs. Dearborn waited stiffly at attention. They were trying to smile and, in Lewis's opinion, not having much success. His father, he was relieved to see, was hairnet-free. Mr. Dearborn looked a bit dull in his navy pants and beige sweater, but at least he wasn't covered in tomato sauce. Mrs. Dearborn, meanwhile, was wearing her "professor" outfit—crisply ironed slacks and a dark jacket. Lewis had been hoping she'd be teaching at the university, but unfortunately she had a spare period this morning.

The first thing that happened was this: Mrs. Dearborn asked everyone to remove their shoes, even though it wasn't raining and nobody's shoes were dirty. Then Mr. Dearborn hung up all the jackets while his wife showed the class the "facilities"—a word some kids didn't understand until they were actually standing in front of the toilet.

Following the crowd, Lewis tried to look on the bright side. What amazing luck that Seth had picked *this* day to get sick! Or play hooky? Lewis didn't know or care which. Hearing the silence when Seth's name was called for attendance, he'd felt light enough to float.

"Well, Mr. Dearborn," said Ms. Forsley with a smile, "shall we begin the tour?"

Everyone turned to Lewis's father, who cleared his throat for such a long time that Lewis's stomach clenched. But when Mr. Dearborn finally started to speak, he sounded almost normal. He sounded, in fact, like a tour guide in a museum.

"Well, boys and girls, the first thing to know is . . . this house is very old. It was built in the 1860s by Captain Jeremiah Douglas, a Scottish merchant who owned a fleet of sailing ships. Jeremiah built Shornoway for his wife, Elizabeth, who he met and married in England. She was just eighteen years old. Think of that! They came here soon afterward. Elizabeth, so the story goes, missed her family very much. Jeremiah built this house for her, on a cliff above the ocean, so that any time she wanted, she could look across the sea toward her home."

"Did it help?" asked a girl named Sarah. "Did it make her feel better?"

Mr. Dearborn looked pleased to be asked. "Nobody knows, my dear. But we do know that Elizabeth Douglas stayed. She made a new home here and had thirteen

180

children. So, I suppose—heh, heh—she missed England less in the end."

"You're right about that," grunted Mrs. Binchy from the edge of the crowd. "With thirteen kids, who'd have *time* to miss England?"

And that's how it went. Mr. Dearborn led the class around the ground floor, offering bits of history that Lewis had never heard before. Ms. Forsley and the kids asked questions, while Mrs. Dearborn followed, surprisingly quiet. Mrs. Binchy tagged along, too, adding wry comments that made everyone laugh.

As for Lewis's father . . . well, Lewis was astounded. As the class straggled up the back stairs, he caught up and whispered, "Dad! How do you know all this stuff?"

"Research," said his father.

"Re—what kind?"

"I'll show you later."

On the second floor, they moved room by room down the hall. Ms. Forsley kept letting out little cries of delight. "Oh my goodness, will you look at this? A coal oil lamp. Must be a hundred years old. And—oh!— look at this commode."

Slowly they worked their way to the end.

And then, they were there—Lewis's whole class, waiting outside Libertalia. Lewis watched as his father slowly turned the doorknob. Mr. Dearborn was saying something, but Lewis's ears had stopped working, and all he could hear was *rowrr-rowrr*, like the slowed-down track of a movie. The door cracked open, sunlight beamed through and the kids filed inside. Lewis followed, holding his breath.

His classmates were looking around. A few turned to stare at him.

"This is your *room*?" said Alex Neeson. "Up here in this tower?"

Lewis nodded.

Alex walked over to the green glass cabinet. He stared at the tin soldiers on top. Then he squatted and peered at the old toys inside. Lewis waited for him to laugh. He waited for Alex to ask, "Don't you have any *real* games?"

But he didn't.

Mike Burrows wandered over to Lewis's desk. "Hey, cool! A ship in a bottle."

Other kids gathered around. Mike asked how the ship got inside.

As Mr. Dearborn started to explain, Lewis searched the room for signs of the pirates. He couldn't *see* them. Nor could he hear their voices. But he was suddenly sure, beyond any doubt . . . *they were there!*

It was the air. It had that unnaturally sharp feeling of coolness. And the fishy odor was strong. But most of all, Lewis realized, he could just . . . tell.

"So you see," said Mr. Dearborn, "the ship-maker attaches the masts and sails to the ship with hinges and strings, so the ship will lie flat and narrow while it's being inserted into the bottle neck . . ."

And that's all Lewis heard because, in the corner of his eye, he spotted the evidence he'd been looking for. One of the lace curtains was moving. Slowly it swelled out, larger and larger, into a shape that was impossible not to recognize. Barnaby Bellows!

Lewis blinked a couple of times, thinking hard. In three quick steps, he was at the middle window. He pulled it open, allowing the wind to come in. If the pirates were going to make the curtains bulge, he could at least provide an explanation.

But the open window began attracting his classmates. They crowded over to stare at the view.

"Aaaaaahhhhh," said a deep, rough voice from their midst, "there ain't nothing on this earth like a good salt breeze."

Lewis froze.

Crawley!

He was right in the middle of Lewis's classmates. Invisible.

"Why, yes, indeed!" replied Mr. Dearborn heartily. "Quite right! A good salt breeze is one of the great pleasures of a home like Shornoway." He didn't seem to know—or care—who had spoken.

And to Lewis's astonishment, no one *else* wondered about the voice, either. Nor did anyone notice when a tin soldier rose quietly off the green cabinet and began moving slowly across the room. But, of course, no one else was *looking* for such things.

So no one except Lewis noticed when Mrs. Dearborn suddenly twitched in an odd way and looked down at her jacket—where her pocket showed a small bump. Reaching inside, she pulled out . . . the tin soldier.

Her mouth dropped open. But she didn't speak. She just stared at the toy for a very long time, her forehead crinkled.

Her husband, meanwhile, was concluding his explanation of the eight-sided construction of the tower. "Any other questions?" he asked the group.

Amanda Wilcox put up her hand. "Is Shornoway . . ." She paused nervously. "Haunted?"

Lewis held his breath.

Ms. Forsley shook her head. "Excuse me, Amanda, that's not really a polite—"

"No, no." Mr. Dearborn held up a hand. "It's all right." He smiled at Amanda. "I'll bet you heard that from someone, didn't you?"

She nodded. "My grandma."

"Well," said Mr. Dearborn, "sometimes, over the years, old houses get that reputation, whether they deserve it or not. Especially if they become rundown and start to look—heh, heh—spooky. Makes them more interesting, I suppose."

"Folks love a good story, " sniffed Mrs. Binchy, frowning at Amanda. "You tell your grandma for me—Irene Cotter, isn't it?—that she doesn't need to be wasting people's time with silly rumors. You tell *Irene* that if there *were* ghosts here, I'd have sent them packing long ago."

Ms. Forsley spoke up quickly. "Thank you, Mrs. Binchy. I think we've had enough talk of ghosts. We don't want to scare Lewis, do we?" She gave him a joking smile.

He tried to smile back, but his mouth felt as if it had been frozen at the dentist.

"Is this where she stared out to sea?" asked Abbie. "The bride? Elizabeth Douglas?"

She was standing by the window alone, with the breeze lifting her long dark hair. "Is this where she looked home to England?"

"I imagine it was," said Mr. Dearborn softly.

The whole class stared at Abbie, framed by the window, her long hair drifting in the breeze. It was as if they had traveled back in time to catch a glimpse of young Elizabeth Douglas, longing for her family across the sea.

Finally, Mrs. Binchy broke the spell. "Who's hungry?" The class thundered down to the dining room.

Food had been laid out across a white linen tablecloth on the giant table. There was, Lewis was delighted to see, no sign of goat cheese anywhere. No eggplant, squid or snails, either. Instead, there were large platters of tiny triangular sandwiches filled with salmon and egg salad and shaved roast beef. Tiny quiches awaited, too—still warm, with soft, flaky crusts. And that was just *one* end of the table. The other was crowded with desserts—lemon tarts, cranberry squares, caramel-pecan clusters. To wash the feast down, there were huge pots of tea—raspberry, mint and regular—served in delicate china cups.

"Ohhh," said Ms. Forsley, when she saw the spread. "How wonderful! Like an old English teahouse."

Lewis's mother, who had been very quiet, spoke up now. "We're lucky to have *two* fine cooks at Shorno-way," she said. "Mrs. Binchy and my husband. I hope you'll all enjoy their excellent food. There are plenty of napkins at the end of the table, children. I'm sorry, but I have to leave you now."

Ms. Forsley offered thanks, and Lewis was surprised to see that his mother still looked a bit stunned.

He was even more surprised when he spotted the bump in her pocket. She was still carrying the tin soldier! He saw her pat her pocket as she left for the university.

Shaking his head in bewilderment, he turned back to the food. He was far too excited to eat, but he put a couple of sandwiches on a plate. Then he stood beside Ms. Forsley, so he could hear her exclaim as she popped things into her mouth,

"Really," she said to Mr. Dearborn, "you could run a great teahouse. This food is amazing!"

"Didn't I say so?" Mrs. Binchy nudged Lewis's father. "If I've told him once, I've told him a hundred times, he could have crowds flocking here. Taught him everything I know about cooking. Not that I take *all* the credit. He has the gift." Offering a bowl of sweet pickles to Ms. Forsley, she added, "A teahouse is fine, but *I've* always said it should be a bed-and-breakfast. All these rooms, sitting empty. It's a shame."

Ms. Forsley turned to Lewis's father. "Have you ever thought of that, Mr. Dearborn? Turning Shornoway into . . . well, an inn or a teahouse or a bed-and-breakfast?"

Lewis almost choked on his sandwich. Here— here!—was the answer to Shornoway's problems.

But Mr. Dearborn just shrugged. His face got that hopeless smile Lewis recognized from the book writing.

"I'm not a businessman. There's a lot more to running an inn than cooking. It's a nice idea, but *look* at this place." He gestured at the stained wallpaper. "It would cost a fortune to restore. I'm afraid we don't have that kind of money."

"But surely," said Ms. Forsley. "Forgive me, it's none of my business, but . . . your inheritance?"

Mr. Dearborn sighed. "The inheritance is only the house. There's almost no money."

The sandwich in Lewis's mouth glued itself dully to his teeth.

Mrs. Binchy nodded sadly. "It's a shame. Wonderful old place like this, coming down."

"Coming down?" Ms. Forsley's eyes widened in alarm.

Lewis couldn't listen anymore. He ran to the bathroom and stayed there, sitting on the edge of the tub, till he heard the kids leave.

Mrs. Binchy and his father were clearing up when he returned.

"Ah, there you are," said Mr. Dearborn. "We wondered where you'd got to. Your classmates have already gone back. I said I'd drive you over after lunch."

"Lunch?" said Mrs. Binchy. "Look at these empty plates. I'd say lunch is over for today."

Lewis smiled. "It was great, Mrs. Binchy, Dad.

Really good food. The kids liked it. Thank you."

He realized, as he said it, that it was true. Somehow, the class visit *had* turned out all right.

His father looked pleased. "What about my speech? Was it okay?"

"The speech was great."

"Would you like to see my research now?"

Lewis wasn't in the mood, but his father had done so much. He followed Mr. Dearborn to his study.

His father handed him a thin, faded book. "I found this in the library."

The cover said *Tandy Bay, A History* by Edmund William McAlistair.

"There are McAlistairs in my school," said Lewis, opening the book. It didn't look like a real book. The pages had been typed on a typewriter, instead of printed. The cover looked homemade.

"They're probably relatives of this fellow," said Mr. Dearborn. "This book was written in 1938. McAlistair published it himself, just a few copies apparently. Still, it's quite well done. It seems he was a history buff. Like me. Heh, heh."

Lewis flipped through.

"Shornoway's on page 52," said his father. "A whole chapter. I don't know where McAlistair got his information, but it looks authentic."

Lewis found the Shornoway section. There was an old photo of a building that he recognized as Shornoway, except that the house in the picture was bright and elegant, with no broken windows or sagging eaves. Surrounded by well-kept shrubs and lawns, it looked grand and stately, with the tower giving it a castle-like air. Glancing through the paragraphs, Lewis found the part about Elizabeth and Jeremiah Douglas.

"There's another bit you might enjoy in this book," said his father. "About the pirates who used to sail this coast."

"Pirates?" The back of Lewis's neck prickled.

"It mentions the *Maria Louisa*. That's the ship they restored—the one down in the museum. Did you know that it ended its days as a pirate ship?"

Lewis had to work to get his voice under control. "Dad? May I borrow this book?"

His father looked pleased. "Of course. Just be careful. The pages are fragile."

Lewis hurried to the parlor, where he dropped onto a sofa and started flipping through the book. It took just a minute to find it.

The printing was faded and uneven but still readable. It said that a notorious pirate, Captain Dire, had attacked the *Maria Louisa* in the waters just off

Tandy Bay. At the time of the attack, the *Maria Louisa* was sailed by another crew of pirates, led by a Captain James Crawley. Crawley's nickname, Lewis learned, had been "Gentleman Jim."

```
Crawley was known up and down the coast
by this name because of his tendencies
to softheartedness and his habit of
sparing the lives and even the for-
tunes of those he attacked. Crawley
himself disliked the name intensely,
preferring to think of himself as
fierce and ruthless. He forbade his
crew to ever use it in his presence.
```

Lewis let out a loud snort. Then he read on.

```
The other captain, Dire, was far from
gentlemanly. He was as cruel a pirate
as had ever sailed the seas, and he
spared no one—not even children.
```

```
On the day that he captured the Maria
Louisa, he keelhauled the navigator,
Harry Douglas, just for sport and would
have tortured the others, too, except
```

that a storm was coming. He contented himself with hog-tying the entire crew with a single rope, claiming they were "not worth two," and then he hurled them overboard. Tied together, Crawley's men sank like stones. Captain Dire sailed away on the captured *Maria Louisa*.

But in a strange twist of fate, Dire himself died, less than three months later, of food poisoning. Most of his crew, having shared the same tainted beef, died with him.

Lewis closed the book and took a deep breath. A smile crept across his face.

He was right! Crawley *wasn't* the awful, wicked criminal he claimed to be.

Gentleman Jim!

Lewis grinned and jumped up, ready to take the book straight to the pirates. He would read it out loud to them. What would Crawley say?

He was halfway up the stairs, when he stopped. After all these years, what difference did it make?

He carried the book to his father's office. "Thanks, Dad."

"Interesting, isn't it?" said Mr. Dearborn. "About Gentleman Jim."

Lewis laughed.

His father gave him a quizzical look. "What's so funny?"

"Nothing," said Lewis. "Nothing."

He waited till he was in the hall to laugh again. He laughed for a long time, muffling the sound with his hands.

21

At school that afternoon, Lewis could feel the kids staring. But it felt okay.

"Hey, Dearborn," said Justin at recess. "You always eat that way in your house?"

Lewis thought about the sautéed kidneys he had left on his plate a week earlier. "No," he said. "Not always."

"Did you bring any leftover desserts?"

"Just one." Lewis realized suddenly that he should have brought more. "A lemon tart. Do you want it?"

Justin shook his head. "Nah, you keep it. If there's just one."

It wasn't a *big* thing, talking to Justin. And it wasn't

a big thing when, a little later, Olivia asked where he'd gotten the ship in the bottle. But something in Lewis that had been tight as a fist felt a little bit looser. They had come to his house. They had seen everything—well, almost everything—and they hadn't mocked or sneered.

The next day, Seth returned.

Lunch hour was almost over, and Lewis was finishing a granola bar in the schoolyard, when it came—a sharp poke in his side, right where the bruise had been.

He didn't move.

"Hey, Lewisssssssser. You're standing in my square again."

Stepping in front of Lewis, Seth leaned in so close, their faces almost touched. Seth's skin was tight, flushed a hot red. The other guys weren't with him. Lewis suddenly wanted those other guys.

"So what, Dearborn? You think you're so great now? Even MORE special, with your big house and your ape-man bodyguard? Think I'm scared?"

Seizing Lewis by the hair, Seth forced his head down. "See? This square here! Take a good look. MINE!" He gave Lewis a shove. "MOVE!"

Lewis lurched backward, but remained in the square. It wasn't that he *planned* to stay there. His body just hadn't figured out where to go.

"You're mean!" said a voice, coming from waist-high.

Lewis glanced down. Two little girls were standing to his right. They looked like kindergartners. One of them, wearing round red glasses that had slid halfway down her nose, was glaring at Seth.

"It's not *your* square," she told him.

Seth grunted. "Bug off, kid."

"*You* bug off." She pushed the glasses higher on her nose. The lenses were thick and covered in fingerprints. Her eyes swam like minnows behind them.

"MOVE, Dearborn!" ordered Seth again.

"It's a free world!" said the girl, plopping her fists on her hips.

As Lewis looked down, a laugh bubbled up in his throat. The little girl was so fierce. He wasn't sure why this struck him as hilarious—why so many things were suddenly striking him as hilarious—but there was no way to stop the laughter that was rising in his chest like lava in a volcano. It rolled out, getting bigger and louder every second.

"Last warning, Dearborn," muttered Seth.

The little girl clamped her lips together. Taking two quick steps, she joined Lewis inside the square.

"There!" she told Seth.

The other little girl, watching all this, let out a giggle. Then *she* stepped into the square, too. Now there

196

were three of them—Lewis and two little girls he'd never seen before. This struck him as funnier than ever. He was howling now. A crowd was gathering.

"MOVE!" yelled Seth.

Suddenly, the small square got even more crowded as a fourth body stepped inside. A tall one.

Abbie.

A long moment followed during which nobody moved. Lewis was still gasping a last few laughs.

"What's going on here?" It was Mrs. Reber.

The girl with the glasses pointed at Seth. "He's being mean."

Mrs. Reber turned to Seth, but he was already loping away. "Okay, everyone, lunch is over. Bell's about to go."

Lewis spent his afternoon in a daze. No matter how often he replayed the schoolyard scene, he came no closer to understanding what had happened.

Abbie caught up as he walked home from school. "Good trick with Seth!" she said. "It worked."

"What trick?"

"The laughing."

Lewis shook his head. "It wasn't a trick."

"Who are the little girls?"

Picturing their upturned faces, Lewis grinned. "I don't know!"

They walked on in silence.

When Abbie spoke again, it was in a whisper. "So where were the you-know-whos? When we visited your house?"

"The pirates?"

"No, the mice. Of *course*, the pirates! Were they behind the red door?"

"They were . . . around. Yeah, that's where they come from—behind the red door. But they seem to like my room the best."

Abbie grunted. "Who wouldn't? You only have the best room in the world."

"I do?" Of course, *he* knew it, but he didn't expect it of other people.

"Are you kidding? Your own tower?"

He smiled. But the smile faded as he remembered that soon the tower wouldn't be there. The whole *house* wouldn't be there.

"So," said Abbie, "have you finished *Treasure Island* yet?"

"Not yet. We're on chapter 26."

"Hey, I'm almost caught up."

They walked on in silence.

"Must be fun," said Abbie, "reading it to real pirates. Seeing how they react, I mean. Knowing they actually lived like that."

"It *is* fun," said Lewis, thinking for the first time

how different it would be to read *Treasure Island* alone. Glancing sideways, he caught the wistful look on Abbie's face.

"Would you like to read *with* us?" He blurted it without thinking.

"Really?" She beamed like a sunrise. "You and the pirates?"

"I'd have to ask them, of course. I don't know how they'd feel. But you've already met Captain Crawley, so I don't see why—"

"Oh, Lewis!" Suddenly, she was hugging him. Her thin arms wrapped tightly around his neck, and her hair brushed his nose. It smelled like lemons.

Just as quickly, she stepped away. "Do you think I could? Really? When?"

Lewis was still flustered by the hug. "Well . . . I don't know . . . I'll ask them and—"

"Doesn't matter. Any time. Oh, Lewis!"

He thought she was going to hug him again, but she hugged herself instead.

"Will you ask the pirates right away?"

"Sure. Tonight. I promise."

It was only when she was walking away that he began to think it through. Was he crazy? The pirates could whip out their swords, they could flash their knives, they could . . .

He took a slow, deep breath. It will be okay, he told himself. He could do this. So could Abbie. So could the pirates. He stared up at the tower and took another breath. It would be okay.

"You invited the *girrrrl?*" shouted Crawley, his face mottled with anger. "Does you think we're a show, lad? Does you think we're a *play* for your friends to come see?"

"No," said Lewis. "I just—"

"Keep the girl away!" snarled Jack the Rat. "We doesn't trusssst her."

"Aye!" hollered Bellows, waving an enormous finger under Lewis's nose. "We wants no girrrrls in Libertalia."

"No strangers, neither," added Moyle.

Lewis threw up his hands. "What are you talking about? I just brought a whole *class* full of strangers into the tower. Girls, too! You were here when they came. Don't tell me you weren't!"

"That were different," said Crawley with a sniff. "We was invisible. We was practicing!"

Lewis let out a sigh.

"Look," he said, "Abbie isn't a stranger. She's my friend. She's already reading *Treasure Island* and—"

"No, by thunder!" roared Crawley. "We don't allow no girls aboard ship, and we won't allow one in Libertalia now!"

"No!" echoed the others. "No!"

Lewis had to shout to be heard. "Excuse me! EXCUSE ME!"

They stopped.

"I think you're forgetting something," said Lewis. "I'll be doing you a big *favor* on Halloween, right?"

The pirates blinked.

"I did you another favor when I bought you those clothes."

Silence. Skittles nodded.

"In fact, I do you a favor every night, don't I? When I read?"

Most of them were staring at the floor now. Even Crawley looked abashed.

"So I think," concluded Lewis, "that it's only fair for you to do *me* a little favor."

"Fair," grumbled Jack. "I hates fair."

There was a mumble of agreement, but it petered out.

Crawley scratched the stubble on his pockmarked chin. "One time!" he said finally. "She can come here one time only. And she takes us as we are, mind. Rough as old rope. You tell her that!"

"I will," said Lewis. "I promise."

The bell rang for dinner. As he walked to the door, he heard a final mutter from Jack. "We'll feed her to the sssharks."

"You will not!" said Lewis over his shoulder.

Jack mumbled something else, too low for Lewis to hear.

There weren't any sharks anyway, thought Lewis. Were there?

He shook his head. The pirates really *were* making him crazy.

22

The part of *Treasure Island* that Abbie wanted to read with the pirates was the end.

"It's hard to wait," she said as she and Lewis left school the next day. It was becoming a habit, this walking partway home together. "But there's something special about finding out how a story ends. Unless . . . do you think I could visit more than once?"

"No," said Lewis quickly. "Sorry." He didn't say how hard it had been to arrange even once.

"Is there anything I should . . . you know, do? Say? When I meet them?"

Lewis heard the tremor in her voice.

"Not really. I'm sure they'll like you." He wasn't sure at all. "Just watch out for Jack the Rat. Try not to get too close."

"Why not?"

He wants to feed you to the sharks, thought Lewis.

"Jack's . . . different."

"Oh," said Abbie. "Okay."

"And you have to take them as they are," he added.

"What does that mean?"

"They're not very . . . polite."

"Oh. Well, what does *that* mean?"

He shook his head. "You'll see for yourself."

In the days that followed, Lewis read steadily with the pirates, while Abbie read the same chapters alone. Seeing that the final two chapters of *Treasure Island* were short, they decided to leave both for her visit.

Lewis, meanwhile, wondered how to explain Abbie's visit to his parents. She solved that problem in a second.

"Just tell them we're working on a project together. We *are*, aren't we?"

When Lewis told his father and Mrs. Binchy about the project, they sounded pleased.

"Invite her for dinner, why don't you?" said Mrs. Binchy. "You'll think better with a good meal in you."

"Yes, of course," said Mr. Dearborn. "We'll plan something delicious."

On the day of Abbie's visit, she walked to Shornoway with Lewis after school. He had decided to leave the tower for after dinner, but he wasn't sure what to do till then. Abbie made that choice herself by lingering in the kitchen, where Mr. Dearborn and Mrs. Binchy were cooking Spanish paella. Lewis had eaten this before—a pan of yellow rice, dotted with chicken, sausage and clams. He watched Abbie, wondering if she'd find it weird.

"Can I help?" she asked.

"Of course you can, lovey," said Mrs. Binchy. "Here! Top these beans."

Lewis, feeling useless, found himself volunteering as well. When Mrs. Dearborn poked her head in fifteen minutes later, there were four people chopping and frying.

"What's all this?" she asked. "Looks like the kitchen at the Ritz."

Mrs. Binchy sniffed. "As if there's anything at the Ritz to match *my* paella."

To Lewis's surprise, his mother sat down and accepted a glass of wine. She didn't join the cooking party, but she did listen—even smiling now and then—to the conversation, most of which came from

Mrs. Binchy. Lewis noticed that, while Mrs. Binchy did most of the talking, it was his father who did the work.

Dinner was perfect. Abbie said it twice. Mr. Dearborn said Abbie was the perfect guest. Lewis was glad to hear the food was good because *he* was so nervous, he could barely taste it. All he could think about was the pirates, upstairs waiting for "the girrrrl."

"Run along now," said Mrs. Binchy when Abbie offered to help clear up. "Homework's more important."

"What's the project, Lewis?" asked Mrs. Dearborn.

Before Lewis could think, the word slipped out. "Pirates."

Abbie's eyes widened.

"Pirates?" Mr. Dearborn reached for the newspaper. "Is it a history project, then? About the pirates along this coast?"

Lewis paused, eyes locked with Abbie's. "Uh-huh."

"Great idea!" Mr. Dearborn snapped open the paper's front section. "You should look at that book again—by that fellow, McAlistair."

"Be sure to write a clear outline," added Mrs. Dearborn. "It makes all the difference."

Lewis and Abbie laughed all the way up the back stairs.

Then they stopped. Suddenly . . . there it was. Lewis

reached out to touch the carved letters on the door. *Libertalia.*

"Ready?" he said.

"I think so."

He knocked twice. Then he opened the door.

The pirates were lined up, waiting. They looked . . . different.

It was their hair! They'd slicked it down. The tangled thatches of the day before had been flattened into greasy-looking manes. Several pirates wore colorful bandanas, tied at the backs of their heads like caps.

And their feet! They were all wearing shoes. Lewis recognized the odd footwear as the contents of an old trunk down the hall. Some of it didn't fit—slippers that barely covered Bellows's toes, enormous rubber boots on Skittles's small feet. But the pirates had all made an effort to cover their gnarled toes and ragged toenails.

They had taken care with their clothing, too. The effect was still ridiculous. But knowing them as he did, Lewis understood that they had put careful thought into those capri pants and satin vests and—in Jack's case—plaid boxer shorts.

"Hi," said Lewis awkwardly, as the silence grew. "This is . . . Abbie."

Heads bobbed stiffly along the row. Captain Crawley, resplendent in a burgundy velvet jacket and green jogging pants, bowed deeply from the waist. "We be most honored, miss."

If Abbie was shocked by the pirates, she didn't show it. She responded with a deep, low curtsy as elegant as if she'd been curtsying all her life.

"Pleased to meet you," she said.

No reply came, except anxious, aching glances. The pirates seemed hypnotized by Abbie. Lewis remembered that although they had *seen* girls over the years, including his mother, and more recently his classmates, they hadn't actually *talked* to any for a very long time. Maybe since they'd died! Even Jack the Rat was wringing his hands with the strain.

What must it be like not to talk to a girl for two centuries? Watching the pirates, Lewis realized that he was looking at a shyness as deep as any he had ever felt. It made him want to help.

"Why don't we sit down?" he said.

There was a flurry as the pirates all reacted at once, stumbling into one another and fighting for the same places on the floor. Captain Crawley smacked several of them aside in his haste to reach the wicker chair, which he dusted off and set in the middle of the rug.

"For you, miss," he said.

"Thank you," said Abbie, settling herself in the chair.

Lewis was astounded. There she sat, surrounded by dead pirates, her smile so comfortable it was as if they were all old friends.

"Well, Lewis?" she said. "Aren't you going to read?"

Taking a seat on the brass bed, he began. He read haltingly at first, aware of Abbie listening, but gradually he relaxed. Soon he was doing the different voices and speaking softer or louder as the words demanded. In this chapter, the treasure was finally discovered, and even though many of the book-pirates perished searching for it, Lewis's pirates were thrilled. They beat on the floor with their fists, hollering "Yo ho!" and before Lewis could stop them, they were punching each other, too. He had to shout for order. Remembering Abbie's presence, the pirates quieted down.

He finished the second-last chapter to a dead hush. The audience waited expectantly.

Lewis offered the book to Abbie. "Would you like a turn?"

The pirates let out a collective gasp.

"Me?" said Abbie.

"Sure!" Lewis focused his gaze on the ghosts, daring them to interfere.

"Well," she said nervously. "If nobody minds."

She started softly. But soon, like Lewis, she was deep into the story, reading with eagerness and expression. When she got to the part where Long John Silver's final fate was described—his mysterious disappearance to an unknown place—the pirates began chanting. "Sil-ver! Sil-ver! Sil-ver!"

Abbie waited, smiling, till they were done, then read the final paragraphs of *Treasure Island*. Slowly, carefully, deliberately, she closed the book.

"Ah, missy," said Crawley after a pause, "the life of a pirate is a raw and perilous thing, and no mistake. The lubber what wrote that book, he knowed it like he was there."

The reading had put the pirates in a pensive mood, but it didn't last. Soon they were engaged in their usual activities—singing, dancing, gambling. Abbie watched, fascinated. She moved her chair over by the window, and the pirates kept their distance—all except Adam, who crept close and settled shyly at her feet. Seeing the eagerness on the cabin boy's face and the quickness with which he began a conversation, Lewis hung back and played a game of cards with Jonas.

It was much too soon when Abbie asked, "What time is it, Lewis?"

The pirates weren't used to saying good-bye any

more than they were used to saying hello. As Abbie thanked them, they mumbled and stared at their feet. Lewis had the feeling that, dazzled as they'd been by her presence, they were also glad to see her leave.

"I'll walk you partway," he said when they got downstairs.

Streetlights glowed on the rain-slicked road.

"Thank you," said Abbie. "I'll never forget it. Or them."

"I know. Sorry they were so shy. They're not usually like that. But at least you got a chance to talk to Adam."

"Uh-huh." She turned to face him. "Lewis, if I tell you a secret, will you promise not to pass it on? To anyone? Especially not the pirates?"

He shrugged. "Okay. Yes, I promise."

"Adam's a girl."

Lewis opened his mouth, but nothing came out. Finally, he managed to croak, *"What?"*

"It's true," said Abbie. "He told me. Well, *she* told me. She said she had a terrible, cruel father. Lewis, it's an awful story. He beat her! She was desperate and ran away to sea. But the only way a girl could be hired on a ship in those days was to pretend to be a boy."

"B-but that was ages ago," spluttered Lewis. "All these years . . . why hasn't she told them?"

Abbie shook her head. "Did you see the way they treated me? As if I were some kind of . . . statue or princess or something? They have funny ideas about girls, Lewis. They're very old-fashioned."

It was not the word Lewis would have chosen. But remembering their first reaction to "the girrrl," he could see she was right.

"She was desperate for another girl to talk to. That's why she told me."

Lewis swallowed hard. "What's his . . . her real name?"

"Mary. Mary Baker. She had nine brothers and sisters, can you believe it?"

"I'm still trying to believe she's a girl," said Lewis.

He shook his head. Here was another enormous idea to wrestle into his brain. He'd been doing so much of that lately. Nothing was what it seemed. Nothing stayed the same.

Then he remembered how he and Abbie had laughed earlier. That was another change—the laughing.

He liked *that* part. The laughing part was good.

23

The week before Halloween was calm. Maybe too calm. Maybe "calm" was the problem.

At school, Abbie talked to Lewis regularly now, as if it were normal. She looked for him in the schoolyard and wandered over, bringing her friends along. She invited him to play kickball three days in a row. On the third day, he said yes. He didn't play well. But he wasn't embarrassingly awful, either.

Seth kept his distance. He continued to scowl and mutter insults. But Lewis, who had received much worse from Jack, was almost able to ignore Seth.

Up in the tower, the pirates were bickering. They fought about their costumes till some of the garments got ripped apart, leading to a confiscation of all thrift store clothing by Crawley. Lewis could see that the end of *Treasure Island* had left them restless. He found a new book of pirate stories in the library, but it wasn't the same. The loss of Long John Silver was felt powerfully. The crew talked about him as if he were a real person.

"Where does you think Long John is now?" asked Jonas one evening. "Where does you suppose that mysterious place is, where he went at the end of the book?"

"China Seas," said Moyle.

"Spanish Main," said Skittles.

"No," said Adam in a strong, certain voice. "He's headed Madagascar way. Long John's in Libertalia."

"Libertalia!" agreed the others. It built into a shout. "LIBERTALIA! LIBERTALIA!"

"Aye," said Crawley, patting Adam's shoulder. "That's where he'll be. Libertalia. And Hook'll be there, too."

"They'll set anchor in the same port," said Bellows.

"Aye!" cried the others.

Lewis stared. They really *believed* it.

Crawley, unfortunately, was doing very little to soothe his crew's nerves. Every day, he got more excited about seeing his ship again.

"Going home, mateys!" he shouted, rubbing his

palms together. "We's been landlubbers long enough. Going home!"

As for Lewis, the closer *he* got to Halloween, the more he began to focus. Seven dead pirates and one jittery boy trying to cross Tandy Bay . . . how many things could go wrong? For the first time, he began to understand Crawley's need for "a plan." For the first time, he began to actually think things through.

It was already settled, of course, that the pirates would be visible. There was no guarantee they could stay *invisible* even if they tried, so Lewis had to count on Halloween. If there was any day in the year when they could walk around looking like themselves, it was October 31.

The question was—what time of day? He had always thought nighttime would be best. But he had discovered, in recent days, that the pirates' biggest fear was car headlights at night.

"Owl's eyes!" said Skittles in a wobbly voice. "Like the owl of hell, flying right at yer. It ain't natural."

We'll go in daylight, decided Lewis. Again, he'd have to count on Halloween. People enjoyed dressing up in Tandy Bay. There should be plenty of odd-looking people roaming around during the day.

The other problem was the size of the group. It would be impossible to travel in a clump-of-eight along the narrow edge of Muckanutt Road. The pirates would have to walk single file.

Did they know *how* to walk single file?

He organized a practice. Back and forth along the upstairs hallway he walked, with Crawley's crew following in a sloppy, trailing line. They *seemed* to get the idea. Some even got into the spirit of it, marching like soldiers. But that didn't mean they'd get it right on the road.

The plan was full of risk. Lewis knew that. But at least it was a plan.

He spelled out the details to Crawley: visible, daytime, thrift store clothing, single file.

"Awwr, now," cried Crawley, "that's a *grand* plan, laddie! And a bold 'un, too. I always knew you had it in you. Didn't I say so, Bellows?"

After that, they waited. October crept to its end.

On October 30th, with one day left till the journey, Lewis took a detour to the drugstore on his way home from school. Searching the Halloween section, he chose a ready-made costume for himself—Frankenstein. There would be dozens of Frankensteins on the streets. But more than that, he hoped the tattered clothing, along with the ghoulish makeup and neck bolts ($3 extra), would help him blend in with his companions.

When he arrived home, drugstore bag in hand, he was surprised to find his father waiting at the door.

"Oh, Lewis! Thank goodness you're home." Mr. Dearborn jerked his son inside and slammed the door behind him.

"What's the matter, Dad?"

"I don't want to scare you." His father *was* scaring him, as he double-locked the door and secured the chain. "Do you remember that strange fellow I saw the other day? I was going out a few hours ago to pick up some shrimp—and suddenly there was *another* fellow, just as odd, coming up the driveway! Could have been his brother. But this one was angry!"

Lewis's skin tingled. "What . . . what did he look like?"

"Furious!" Mr. Dearborn's breath came faster at the memory. "In a rage! He charged at the house, shouting and shaking his fists. He was about to *attack* me! I slammed the door, of course, and called the police. Thank goodness Mrs. Binchy was at her sister's. Her day off today. But then I started to worry about *you* and whether—"

"You called the *police*?"

"Of course! The man was deranged! Children were coming home from school. Why, you yourself could have—"

"I'm fine, Dad. Honest! What did this guy *look* like? How do you know he wasn't the same one as before?"

"This fellow was older," said Mr. Dearborn, "and much more aggressive! He had a black patch over his eye, like the one Abbie brought that time. She's such a nice girl, Lewis, I hate to ask . . . but do you think this fellow has anything to do with her? Didn't she say that eye patch was for her uncle?"

"No," said Lewis, feeling increasingly desperate. "No, not *her* uncle. It was—oh, gosh, Dad, listen—I have to go!"

He ran for the back stairs.

The pirates were in the tower when he got there— visible, as they generally were these days. But the usual chatter and jostling were missing. All eyes were fastened on Crawley.

The captain sat hunched in the wicker chair, as still and as silent as a coiled snake. His face was flushed and mottled, his right eye glazed.

Lewis approached him warily.

"Captain Crawley?"

He had to say it twice.

"Ah . . . laddie . . ."

"What's going on? My father saw you outside today. Where did you go?"

Crawley turned a rheumy eye his way. "Some busyness of my own," he muttered in a low, pained voice. "A matter of . . . private concern."

Lewis blinked in confusion. What possible business could Crawley have out in the world?

"But what—" he began.

"Private!" snarled Crawley, half-rising from the chair. "Does ye not understand PRIVATE?"

Lewis stepped backward. "Yes, sure. Fine. It's not my business."

The captain coiled himself up again and stared morosely at the floor. Lewis turned to the others, a questioning look on his face.

"Best leave the captain be," whispered Moyle.

"Lost in the doldrums," added Jonas.

"I see," said Lewis, who didn't see at all. "Does anyone know . . . what's wrong?"

The pirates shook their heads so quickly, he knew they were telling the truth.

"Maggoty meat," muttered Crawley. "Monstrous rot, putrid flesh, festering swill . . ."

"He'll be right as rain in the morning," whispered Skittles.

Lewis didn't know what to think. *"Will* he be all

right?" he asked. "Will he? Tomorrow morning, we leave for the museum. Everyone has to be ready."

He turned to stare directly at the captain."EVERY-ONE," he repeated, louder than he'd intended.

Slowly, the captain raised his head. He stared at Lewis for a long, tense moment. Then he let out a hollow laugh.

"Ah, yes, young master with the plan. Don't you fret now, I'll be ready. Ready with golden bells on. There ain't nothing in this whole wicked world could stop James Crawley from boarding the *Maria Louisa* tomorrow. NOTHING! Not even—"

He stopped, his face tight, his lips curled back in a snarl. Like a wolf's, thought Lewis.

Crawley gazed around the room, staring at the pirates one by one. Then he rose to his feet and thrust his left fist into the air.

"Am I right, boys? Are we ready? We've waited two hunnert years for this day—and that's two hunnert years too long! We wants our ship!"

The others, hearing this, burst out in chorus. "We—wants—our—ship! We—wants—our—ship! We—wants—our—ship!"

They were on their feet now, all of them—marching, shaking their fists, yelling. Jack and Jonas were pulling out tankards to drink grog that wasn't even there. Bellows was stomping so hard, it was amazing the floorboards didn't crack.

Crawley stood quietly at the edge and watched.

What did it all mean? Was Crawley okay? Was this just a case of last-minute nerves?

There was no way to tell. And no use asking.

Lewis left Libertalia feeling uneasy.

24

Mr. Dearborn was in the kitchen, talking on the phone.

Lewis smacked his forehead. His father! He'd forgotten all about his dad's panic at seeing Crawley outside. Was he phoning the police again?

Lewis tiptoed closer.

Not the police. Lewis heard the words "funding" and "heritage" and "Shornoway." He crept up to the door.

"I appreciate you looking into this, Ms. Forsley," said his father. "It's very kind. Please thank the other members of your society, as well. But I . . . well, I don't see how it's possible." There was a pause. "Yes, I understand. I agree, it's a shame. But, well . . . heh, heh."

A pause, then, "Thank you." He hung up.

"Was that my teacher?" Lewis blurted it from the doorway.

His father jumped. "For goodness sake, Lewis, don't sneak up on me."

"It *was* Ms. Forsley, right? What did she want?"

Mr. Dearborn ran his fingers slowly across his scalp. "Well, she's a member of the local history society, it seems, and she's . . . I suppose she's concerned about Shornoway being torn down."

"SO AM I!" said Lewis. As in the tower, his words came out louder than he'd planned. He seemed to be having trouble with his volume button.

Mr. Dearborn frowned. "What's gotten into you? Come have some dinner. Just you and me tonight. Your mother's at a meeting."

The table was set in the dining room. Mr. Dearborn removed the cover from a casserole. Steam rose in a cloud of savory smells.

"Braised lamb with roasted vegetables. Garlic and shallots—"

But Lewis would not be distracted. "What did Ms. Forsley say?"

Mr. Dearborn sighed and began to serve. "It was about that idea she had of turning Shornoway into an inn. I told her we didn't have the money. But she went off and talked to some people anyway, and she found a . . . well, some sort of foundation that lends money for heritage projects. Converting historical buildings."

"Really?" said Lewis. "So can we do it? Can we turn Shornoway into an inn?"

His father smiled. Lewis wondered how his father's mouth could curve up that way when the rest of his face was doing such a droop. "It's a huge undertaking, Lewis. An enormous risk. Who's to say we'd be any good at running an inn?"

"Maybe we'd be *really* good at it," said Lewis. "All the kids loved the school visit and your speech and . . . and look how well you cook. Look at this!" He poked his fork into the slice of lamb on his plate. "And this." He poked a potato slice. "And this, and this, and this." He poked at a carrot, an artichoke, a giant mushroom. "You'd have Mrs. Binchy to help you— and me, too. I'd help."

"It's not that easy," said his father.

"Easy?" said Lewis. "Nothing's easy." He thought about his struggle to speak at school. He thought about all the years with no friends. He thought about the dead pirates upstairs, and the probably impossible task he faced the next day. "Nothing's *ever* easy, Dad. Nothing I do, anyway."

There was a silence as father and son stared at their plates.

"At least we're not dead yet." Lewis was still thinking about the pirates.

"Dead?" Mr. Dearborn let out a bleat of laughter. "Sorry, Lewis. It was just such a strange thing to say. But you're right. You're *quite* right. We're not dead yet."

As if to prove it, they both took a bite of food.

"How's school?" asked his father.

But Lewis was on a mission. "I don't understand, Dad. You love history, right? Shornoway *is* history. Everyone in Tandy Bay knows that. And Mom's family built it!"

Hearing himself, he paused. "*My* family, actually. My family built Shornoway. Back in the 1800s, like you said."

Which was true, of course. *His* family. *His* history. But he'd never really felt it till that moment.

"It's our home now," Lewis added, not sure his father would understand. "Our *real* home. We should keep it."

Mr. Dearborn put down his fork and knife and gazed at his son quizzically. A smile of genuine pleasure crept across his mouth. "You know what, Lewis? You are really something! You remind me of your great-granddad."

"Good," said Lewis. "That's good."

They continued to eat in silence. Then Mr. Dearborn cleared his throat loudly.

"I'm going to tell you something, Lewis, that may surprise you. Your mother, as you know, is a practical woman. Not given to flights of fancy. But something happened to her on the day of your class visit. I don't know what it was . . . but it had a strange effect. She told me that she felt there was 'something magical' about Shornoway. Something she had felt as a child when she visited here . . . and then forgot. Can you believe that, Lewis? Your mother believing in magic?"

Without waiting for an answer, he continued. "And do you know what? I think I understand what she meant. The fact is, I have felt it myself! It may even have led to this cooking adventure of mine. I don't know how to explain it to you—and I don't suppose you've experienced anything like it yourself, being so young and so busy with your schoolwork—but, honestly, there really *is* something special about this house!"

Lewis tried not to smile. "I think I know what you mean, Dad."

He waited.

His father picked up his fork. He shuffled his vegetables around. Then he stood and paced the room a couple of times. He rubbed his chin. Lewis watched, holding his breath.

Finally, Mr. Dearborn said, "I'm not promising anything."

"I know," said Lewis.

"I don't know whether Charlotte's recent experience will sway her feelings about selling. Your mother can be a tough nut to crack!"

Lewis couldn't help it—he burst out laughing. After a moment, his father joined in.

"Well, it's *true*," said Mr. Dearborn.

"I know, Dad."

"But, perhaps, since you and I both feel so strongly—"

"Do *you* feel strongly?" asked Lewis.

"Of course I do! And your mother cares a great deal about *us*. You and me. Perhaps . . . perhaps she could be talked around."

Lewis nodded. "We'll do it together." He held up his hand for a high five, which he had done several times now at school after kickball games. Mr. Dearborn stared at the hand in confusion, then patted his son's shoulder.

"An inn would be a lot of work," he said.

"I know."

"And we couldn't just jump into it."

"I know."

"We'd have to do a lot of research. Find out what sort of menus other inns offer. Ms. Forsley's probably right about the English tea. It would go over well. My scones are magnificent! And Sunday brunch, of course. I don't know why, but Sunday brunches always seem popular. My eggs Benedict—"

"I know, Dad. Magnificent."

"Well, they *are!*"

His father laughed again. A big laugh this time, not a "heh, heh."

When the dishes were done, Lewis headed upstairs.

The pirates were nowhere to be seen. But judging by the fish smell, they were nearby.

On the floor were seven thrift store outfits. They were laid out neatly in a row and seemed to wait expectantly, like stockings at Christmas.

And that's when he realized, truly and deeply, for the first time . . . this was actually going to happen.

25

Eating his scrambled eggs the next morning, Lewis pondered his first obstacle—getting the pirates out of Shornoway.

They'd been waiting beside his bed when he woke up, clutching their outfits and looking jittery. Skittles and Jonas, more excited than the others, were glowing quite brightly. Lewis had left them to put on their costumes, promising to return when it was time.

And now, as he chewed on his toast, he saw that there were three obstacles to getting the pirates out—and they were right there in front of him in the kitchen. Mrs. Binchy was elbow-deep in suds at the kitchen sink, while his parents sat talking at the table, having only just figured out that it was Halloween.

"I can take Lewis trick-or-treating tonight," said Mr. Dearborn to his wife. "Have you got a costume, Lewis? My goodness, Halloween already."

"I'm not going this year," said Lewis. "Sixth grade is too old."

This was, strictly speaking, not true. Some of his classmates were still trick-or-treating. But not with their *fathers*!

His mother glanced at her watch. "I'd better be off. Enjoy your field trip, Lewis."

Excellent, thought Lewis. Mrs. Dearborn had accepted the "field trip" story he had made up to avoid having to go to school. Staying as close to the truth as possible, he said he was meeting his class at the Maritime Museum at ten.

"Bye, Mom."

Mr. Dearborn stood up. "Must make a few phone calls," he said. "I'll be in my study."

"Take your time!" said Lewis.

He headed for the bathroom to put on his Frankenstein costume. It was simple. Just a tattered black shirt and pants and a rubber headpiece that made his head look tall and square, and (bonus!) covered his red hair. A wire around the back of his neck attached a large metal bolt to each side of his neck.

The makeup took longer. The color was a sickly combination of gray, green and yellow, and as Lewis smeared it on, he was pleased to see how close a match it was to the pirates' skin. Borrowing his mother's eyebrow pencil, he drew a stitched-up wound on his forehead and another on his cheek. Then he used the pencil to darken the areas around his eyes.

He stood back to check the results. Not a *perfect* Frankenstein—he could have done better with more time—but it would do.

He returned to the kitchen, where his father was chatting to Mrs. Binchy as he put on his coat. He seemed to be having a lot of trouble getting his arms through the holes.

"Lewis! Good! You're still here! You'll be happy to hear the news."

Not even noticing the Frankenstein costume, Mr. Dearborn launched in. "I phoned that foundation that Ms. Forsley mentioned—the one that has money to help with historic buildings. She had already spoken to them, wasn't that kind? And they sounded quite *positive*, Lewis. Yes, yes, encouraging. I'm going there now to pick up their information." He nodded eagerly as Mrs. Binchy helped him with the coat. "And your mother . . . well, I *did* speak to her last night. Now, she hasn't exactly said yes. Not exactly. But she did feel it was worth exploring. So what do you think about *that*? I must say, Lewis, I have rather a good feeling about this."

Lewis grinned back, partly in pleasure and partly in amazement. "Me, too, Dad. Good feeling."

Mr. Dearborn gave his body a great shake, and the coat settled onto his shoulders. Making an awkward fist, he gave Lewis a light punch on the arm. "Must go, son. Time waits for no man! Have a good day at the museum."

Lewis was left with Mrs. Binchy.

"Well now," she said, shaking her head. "A foundation. Isn't *that* a lovely turn of events? By the way, Lewis, nice costume!"

"Thank you," he said.

But he wasn't thinking about his costume.

He was thinking about how to get the pirates past Mrs. Binchy. They were so excited. *Glowing* with excitement, in fact. And the housekeeper was so nosy.

"Uh, Mrs. Binchy . . . are you . . . going out this morning?" He crossed his fingers.

"Out?" she said. "Now where would I be going?"

He shrugged. "Shopping?"

"Is there something you need at the store, Lewis?"

"No . . . I just . . . nothing."

She frowned. "What is it? Are you—"

Abruptly, she stopped. She gave him a long, penetrating stare. "It's about *them*, isn't it?"

A long pause followed.

"Them!" she repeated. "*You* know! The pirates in the tower."

Lewis swallowed hard. He forced himself to speak. "You . . . *know* about them?"

"Well now, how would I *not* know? Living and working here all these years with your great-granddad. I'd have to be some kind of idiot."

Lewis could only stand there, swaying. He felt as if he'd been hit by a brick. Mrs. Binchy knew about the pirates?

"Not that I've ever *seen* them," she said. "But I've heard them often enough, and felt them pass by. Back in your great-granddad's day, they wandered all over the house. They've gotten shyer since you lot moved in."

Knees wobbly, Lewis had to sit at the kitchen table.

"Well now," said Mrs. Binchy, softly.

He heard her walk over, felt her hand patting his head. "It's all a bit much, isn't it?"

He gazed up into a round, red face that suddenly looked less silly than it always had.

"Why didn't you say something?" he asked her. All that chattering she did, day after day, and not a word about the pirates.

"Your great-granddad wanted you to get to know them on your own. He said I wasn't to interfere. Of course, I would have stepped in if I thought you were in trouble. But you seemed to be doing fine."

"Fine?" The word surprised him.

"Well, not *totally* fine, of course. But who is? I thought . . . well, I imagined they might be company for you. You seemed so alone. And I knew from the old days with your great-granddad that they were a jolly bunch."

Jolly. Again, not a word Lewis would have chosen. But he knew what she meant.

"I have to go now, Mrs. Binchy," he said. "I have to . . . help them."

She nodded, not surprised. "You're taking them to their ship?"

"Yes."

"I expected as much. So did your great-granddad. He knew you would help."

"I haven't done anything yet," said Lewis. "Today, I hope."

"You picked a good day. All the spirits out and about on All Hallows Eve. Who'd notice a few more?"

"Yes. Well, then . . ." Lewis started to rise to his feet.

"Not quite yet," said Mrs. Binchy. "It may be . . . yes, I think it's right. Before you leave, you should read your great-granddad's letter."

"I don't have time for—WHAT?"

"Your great-granddad wrote you a letter," said Mrs. Binchy. "It was before he went off his head, poor dear. He asked me to keep it and give it to you when I thought the time was right."

"And that's . . . now?" said Lewis.

She nodded. "I'll be right back."

Moments later, she was back, sniffing a small white envelope.

"Smells like your great-granddad," she said with a sigh. "His pipe. Takes me back. Here."

Lewis took the envelope and turned it over. There it was, his name. *Lewis*.

He began to open it, then looked at Mrs. Binchy.

"Oh!" She rolled to her feet. "Don't mind me. I'll start my apple pies."

It was a single sheet, written on both sides in a small, slanted hand.

Dearest Lewis,

If you are reading this letter, then you have met our guests, the crew of the Maria Louisa. I hope you have been of some help to them, and I am equally hopeful that they have been helpful to you. Watching you over these past years, I have often felt that you might benefit from some time with the pirates. They certainly have needed someone like you, Lewis, a healthy young man with a generous heart who could do for them what I could not.

By now, you may have become friends. If so, I thought you might be interested to learn of another connection you have with these long-dead men. Their history is shrouded in mystery to most, but I took an interest and did some research, traveling as far as London and New York to seek answers.

What I learned was this. When the Maria Louisa was captured by a Captain Dire, seven of her crew drowned. These are the seven you have met.

But one of Crawley's crew managed to escape. He was called Laughing Harry, and he was dragged beneath the ship that day as punishment. When he didn't come up, everyone thought he was dead. But the truth was, he managed to free himself.

Badly wounded but still alive, he was carried to shore by the tide. He was the *Maria Louisa's* navigator, and his full name was Harold Gordon Douglas.

Fortunately for him, he was found by kind people on shore, who nursed him back to health. Later, he made his way back to Scotland, where he married and became a merchant. And so, his pirate days ended forever. But along the way, he heard the awful tale of how his shipmates had perished, and he wondered often about fate, and how it had allowed him alone to survive. On the twentieth anniversary of his crewmates' deaths, he returned to Tandy Bay and stood upon the cliffs to pray for them at a church service he had arranged with the village priest.

He stayed only a day or two, but he brought his son with him—a boy named Jeremiah. That boy was struck powerfully by the beauty of Tandy Bay and especially by the majestic view from the cliffs. Jeremiah went home to England with his father, but he never forgot those cliffs. When he grew up, he came back here, and he brought his young English bride with him. Her name was Elizabeth. He built Shornoway for her. They had thirteen children.

Elizabeth and Jeremiah Douglas were my great-great-great-grandparents, Lewis. (There are more greats, no doubt, but this is a small piece of paper.) That means, of course, that they were your ancestors, as well. And so was Harold Douglas.

Yes, Lewis, you and I are direct descendents of Laughing Harry Douglas, the navigator of the *Maria Louisa*. We have a bit of pirate in our blood! I wonder what you think of that.

For myself, I have found that it comes in handy now and then, if properly used, and I hope it will be the same for you. You are a good boy, Lewis, and that's a fine and valuable thing. You have always done exactly what was expected of you. But there are times in life when one must be bold, moments when one must listen to one's heart, rise to its call and dare all. At such moments, a drop of pirate blood may help.

Onward, Lewis of Libertalia!

With love from
Great-Granddad

P.S. Crawley and his crew don't know we are related to Laughing Harry. I have been tempted many times to tell them, but now I leave that pleasure to you.

Lewis stared at the letter, stunned. He had a pirate ancestor. So did his mother! Maybe that explained her bossiness and the oversized voice. He couldn't wait to tell her and his father about Laughing Harry Douglas.

He especially couldn't wait to tell Captain Crawley.

He replaced the letter in the envelope. Standing, he held it out to Mrs. Binchy. "Thank you. Can you keep it for me till I get back?"

She nodded.

"I'll get the pirates now," he said.

They were waiting, dressed in their outfits. Colorful as a bowl of bubble gum, they were standing in a row in a shaft of morning sunlight. Lewis couldn't remember when he'd seen so much . . . brightness!

There was Jonas, pleased and proud in his fuzzy pink tracksuit. Beside him, Jack managed to look nasty even in a frilly white blouse. Bellows stood out as always, his lower half a sea of purple flowers, while Skittles glowed in a tangerine tie-dyed T-shirt. All that was needed to make the picture completely ridiculous was Hawaiian prints (Moyle) and polka dots (Adam).

"Atten-SHUN!" hollered Crawley, hitching up his gold basketball shorts.

To Lewis's surprise, the pirates snapped to attention. Crisp salutes greeted him down the line.

He saluted back uncomfortably. "Er . . . at ease."

As soon as the words were out, they gathered around him.

"Ain't *you* a picture!" said Crawley. "Just what in the name of thunderation is *this*?" He pulled at Lewis's square rubber head. "And what happened to yer skin? Has you been struck by the *plague* since we last saw you, lad?"

"It's makeup," said Lewis. "For Halloween."

"Well, I ain't much acquainted with yer Halloween, but if it makes a lad screw bolts into his neck . . ."

"They're not real, Captain Crawley. It's a costume. Just like yours."

Crawley patted his shorts. "Nay, not like *my* costume. Not like mine at all."

"Course not," said Moyle. "The lad looks like a canker sore!"

"Like a dirty old sausage left out in the rain," added Jonas.

The pirates laughed. All except Crawley.

"ENOUGH!" he shouted. "Leave the lad be. It's time to weigh anchor, mates. The *Maria Louisa* awaits."

He paused to gaze around the tower. Removing his

baseball cap, he placed it over his heart. The other pirates followed suit.

"One last adieu to the old manse afore we departs. She was never our home, to be sure. But she were a sweet place to visit for a few centuries. Say good-bye, mateys, say good-bye. And now, young Lewis . . . lead the way!"

Now that Lewis didn't have to hide the pirates from Mrs. Binchy, he shouldn't have minded their noise as they thundered downstairs. Even so, it was hard not to say "Shush!"

When they reached the ground floor, he looked around for the housekeeper, peeking into the kitchen and calling her name.

She didn't answer, and he couldn't wait. Not with seven dead pirates on his heels.

"This way!" he called, heading for the front door. When he pulled it open, the wind blew him nearly off his feet—a bitter gust that cut right through his clothes.

He shivered and glanced down. His Frankenstein costume was only a thin layer of cotton. Underneath, he was wearing jeans and a T-shirt.

"Wait!" he told the pirates, crowding behind him in the doorway. "I need a jacket."

He pushed his way back to the front hall closet. When he opened the door, she was standing there, huddled between the coats.

"Mrs. Binchy! What are you doing in the closet?"

She tried to smile. "I don't really know, dear. Suddenly, the thought of actually *seeing* them . . . it gave me the willies."

She peeked past him now. "They don't look so bad, do they? Quite colorful . . . if you don't get too close."

Lewis nodded. "I need my jacket, Mrs. Binchy. It's cold outside."

She stepped out of the closet, searched through the coats and pulled out a red plaid jacket. It looked familiar.

"It belonged to your great-granddad," she said, holding it up. "Wear it for luck!"

The jacket was old and ugly. But it was warm, and the red would blend in with the pirates' bright clothes. Lewis pulled it on. It smelled of Great-Granddad's pipe.

"Thanks, Mrs. Binchy. For everything."

She nodded. "Off with you now!"

He pushed through the pirates and led the way outside. As he walked down the front steps, they followed . . . but slowly. He remembered that some had not been outside in decades. He waited as they inched their way down.

Crawley was not so patient.

"Push these yobs along, young Lewis. They could spend a whole week on these stairs."

Lewis laughed and hastened his pace. As he led the crew down the driveway, Mrs. Binchy's treble voice followed.

"Good luck, dear Lewis. Onward!"

26

The wind from the north blew strong, stinging
Lewis's green-hued face and flattening his red
jacket as he led the way down Muckanutt Road. He
glanced back.

They were keeping up. Good! Seven of them in a
wobbly, windblown line, with Crawley at the rear.

Hearing a motor ahead, Lewis tensed. This was
the test.

"Car coming!" he yelled. "Everyone stay calm."

As the car pulled into view, Lewis could see the
driver—a dad-looking guy with a bald head. Spotting
Lewis's costume, he grinned and tapped a couple of
beeps on his horn.

The pirates leaped into a flower bed.

"NO!" yelled Lewis as the car passed. "Wrong!"

He helped them out of the flowers, now crushed and mangled. "It's just a horn," he told them. "Don't be scared."

"WHO'S scared?" hollered Jack, springing forward. "I'll—"

"STOW IT!" yelled Crawley. "Till we reaches the moo-see-um, this *lad* is in charge. You heed his words as you heed mine! Take your place, Jack."

Jack whirled and spat on a mailbox. Then he slunk back into line.

Lewis started walking again. A second car passed, without slowing. The pirate line held firm.

At a curve in the road ahead was the bus stop. Two old ladies in long coats were seated on a bench, their feet dangling. Lewis looked more closely. Weren't these the same old ladies who'd been sitting there when he walked to the thrift store with Crawley?

"Good morning," said Lewis as he approached.

The one in the red hat giggled. "Good morning, Frankenstein," she said.

Then, as the pirates passed, the other one called, "Good morning, ZOMBIES!"

The old ladies clutched each other, shrieking with laughter.

Lewis started laughing, too.

There was a tap on his shoulder. "What's a zombie?" asked Moyle.

You, thought Lewis. What *you* look like. "Zombies are good," he said. "Don't worry."

It was *working.* His plan was actually working.

More cars passed. Every time it happened, the pirates got jittery. A few glowed wildly and yelled and grabbed each other. But they managed to stay in line. And they managed to fool the drivers, who just smiled and waved.

Only the dogs knew. A black lab went berserk when they passed its yard. It came charging up to the fence, hackles raised, barking and whirling in circles.

"Can't fool no dog," muttered Skittles.

"Dudley! Hey, Dudley. Cut it out!" yelled a woman from the porch. "What's gotten into that dog?"

It was a relief to leave Muckanutt Road and get onto Highbury Lane. Walking on the sidewalk, the pirates looked more relaxed—all except Crawley. He continued to brood, his features gloomy. It was as if his mind was somewhere else.

But no time to worry about Crawley. The smaller streets had more pedestrians, and the pirates were attracting attention.

A young guy with a nose ring and a brown leather

jacket gave them a thumbs up. "Hey, cool! *Night of the Living Dead.* I like it."

A woman in a cowgirl costume, pushing her bunny-suited baby, said, "Look, Lucy! Zombies." The baby caught the interest of the pirates—especially Jack the Rat, who stuck his face right into its stroller. The baby wailed for half a block.

"Cut that out," said Lewis.

"Bah!" said Jack. Then his mouth dropped open as he spotted something behind Lewis.

Lewis turned. A gorilla was walking toward them.

Uh-oh, thought Lewis. He turned again. But not in time to stop Jack, who was running at the gorilla with—yes, a dagger!

Fortunately, Crawley chose that moment to start paying attention. As Jack ran past, he reached out and snatched the smaller pirate right off the sidewalk.

Lewis caught up. "It's not a real gorilla, Jack! It's not!"

But the gorilla was a lesson. However well the pirates were behaving, they were still pirates. He needed to get them to the museum quickly, before they could cause *real* trouble.

There were two more dogs on the walk—a growling Rottweiler and a hysterical Chihuahua. Lewis kept the pirates moving. As they neared the municipal center, his heart began to pound. They were almost there. They were going to make it. He had actually led seven ghosts across Tandy Bay!

Then he remembered. The police station. It was right beside the museum. He should check things out before bringing the pirates any closer.

He led them into the museum parking lot and stopped. As they began to mill about, Crawley joined him in three swift strides.

"We're here!" said Lewis. "We did it, Captain Crawley. Can you believe it?"

"Aye, lad, we's arrived. And we thanks you kindly for bringing us."

"Can you wait here for a minute while—"

"No need for that, lad. We travel alone now."

"What?"

"You can go."

"I . . . *what*?" said Lewis.

Crawley narrowed his eye. "Yer work is done, young Lewis. Best for you to go home now."

Lewis was too shocked to speak. After all the work he'd done? The planning, the clothes, the training. And now he was supposed to just . . . go home? Not even see the pirates board their ship?

"But that's not fair," he said. "That's—"

Crawley's face grew hard. "This ain't a right place

248

for you today. There's things as may happen—I'll say no more. Heed my words. Go home!"

"I won't," said Lewis. "I'm coming in, too. You can't stop me."

The captain glared at Lewis so fiercely, it was like being struck. Grabbing the boy by the shoulder, Crawley hauled him away from the others, behind a pay station.

"I didn't want to tell you, sonny," he whispered, "and I didn't want to tell the boys, neither—not till I had to. But you'll find out soon enough. Does you remember how I went exploring yesterday? On me own?"

Lewis nodded. "You frightened my father. He said you were angry."

"Angry don't half say it. The place I went to yesterday was *right here*—to this moo-see-um. I wanted to reconnoiter. Have a look-see. And what did I find inside these walls? Ah, laddie, it were a foul thing. A foul, repulsive thing!"

"What?" asked Lewis.

Crawley's hand curled into a fist. "I could *smell* them the second I comes near! I'd know that smell anywhere. The stench of rotting teeth! Maggoty meat! Dying rats!"

"But what?" begged Lewis. "What was it?"

"Putrid flesh! Festering swill!"

"Captain Crawley! Please! *What* did you find?"

Crawley lifted his gnarled fist into the air and shook it.

"DIRE!" he croaked hoarsely.

"Dire?" repeated Lewis. "You mean . . . Captain Dire? The pirate who stole your ship? Who threw you overboard?"

"Dire, aye! That son of a scab, Dire! Standing there at the helm of *my* ship with his scraggly mane of white hair and those terrible, cold, dead eyes. Those icy blue eyes what can freeze your marrow. It were him, all right. Him and his stinking crew—twelve or more— crawling over the deck like sea lice on a whale. They're here, lad—right *here*, on our sweet little *Maria Louisa*! They been aboard ship all these many years, while we sat landlocked in a tower."

Stunned by this news, Lewis tried to take it in. "Twelve of them? But wait—you're only seven. You're outnumbered! Listen, Captain Crawley, you can't go in there. You have to come back to Shornoway. You—"

Crawley seized him by his jacket and pulled him up so they were face to face. "ARE YE MAD?" boomed the captain. "Back to Shornoway? Wash your mouth out, ye pettifogging little gnat! Two hunnert years and more we've waited for our ship. Are we to give her up now? NO! We stays RIGHT HERE, and we FIGHTS for her!"

He released Lewis and glanced around. The other pirates, hearing the shouting, had gathered in a circle.

"Dire?" they repeated. "Here?"

"AYE!" shouted Crawley, throwing caution to the wind. "That son of a bilge rat, Dire! We're going to toss him into the drink, mates—just as he tossed us. Are ye ready to take back our ship?"

"AYE!" the pirates cried, pulling out their swords. "AYE, AYE, CAPTAIN!"

Crawley yanked out his own sword and brandished it in the air. With an ear-splitting scream, he ran straight for the brick wall of the museum. He hit it—

And disappeared.

The others cheered. In a wild howling rush, they followed. One by one, they hit the wall and faded.

Lewis was left standing there alone.

27

No! Lewis was *not* going home!

Not a chance.

He made his way to the front door of the Tandy Bay Maritime Museum, where a small crowd waited. Little kids, mostly, and a few adults. Lewis edged up closer.

They looked like—yes, they were!—the kindergartners from his school. There was their teacher, Mrs. Sobowski, trying to herd them into a line. A few parent volunteers helped out. The wind was blowing the kids' hair and flapping their Halloween costumes, making them screech with delight. At the edge of the group, Lewis spotted a familiar face— the little girl with the round red glasses, who had stood up to Seth. She was wearing a princess costume.

Lewis glanced around the grounds. He hadn't been here for several years, but he remembered the grassy lawn that sloped from the museum down to the edge of the ocean. It was home now to a couple of replicas of famous historical boats—a Viking longboat and a Haida war canoe.

The big attraction, of course, was the *Maria Louisa*—inside the museum, behind a glass wall, facing the lawn and the ocean.

The kindergarten line stirred as someone came to open the museum doors. The kids edged forward.

Lewis stared at the entrance. A black-and-orange banner above the door read HALLOWEEN IN THE MUSEUM. A small sign in the window said *Admission Fees*. Several lines down, he read, *Students: $1.50*.

Money!

His wallet was in his jacket. His *own* jacket. The one he had left at home.

He shoved his hands into the pockets of Great-Granddad's jacket, hoping to find change. Out came a single green peppermint, fuzzy with lint. He tried his jeans' pockets. Nothing.

A sick feeling hit his stomach. Why hadn't he *thought* of this? Why hadn't he remembered he'd have to pay?

The door opened. With growing desperation, Lewis watched the kindergarten line snake forward.

Something pulled at his sleeve. He glanced around. Then down.

"Hi!" The little girl's eyes were blurry behind her red glasses. "Did you come to see the ship?"

Lewis stared for a second, then nodded.

She held out her hand. "Come on."

She pulled him into the line, five kids from the end. With his heart pounding, he shuffled forward. The kindergarten class, which now included him, continued to move ahead.

"Nice princess costume," he told the girl as they walked through the door.

She let out a snort. "Not a princess. I'm Mary, Queen of Scots."

"Sorry."

The cashier was just ahead. She was wearing a fuzzy orange wig and clown makeup. The walls behind her were covered in decorations—fake cobwebs, cardboard ghosts and witches.

Lewis stared at his feet as they walked past. Another step, another . . .

He was in!

Lewis looked down at the little girl. "Excuse me. I have to do something."

She glanced around. "It's over there," she said, pointing to the men's room.

A laugh burbled up in Lewis. "Yeah, thanks."

He walked quickly to the front of the kindergarten line, still threading its way toward the main exhibit hall. When he reached Mrs. Sobowski, she frowned at him, clearly wondering who he was. That's when he realized that although he hadn't exactly *planned* to skip school, that's what he was doing. Mrs. Sobowski started to speak to him, but a little boy in a Batman costume chose that moment to sit on a velvet museum cord, bringing down the metal stand it was attached to. She turned to help. Lewis darted past.

Entering the exhibit hall, he did a quick visual scan. Everything *looked* normal. But he caught a strong whiff of the familiar fishy odor—along with a new pungent, sour smell.

And, listening hard, he was sure he could hear muffled thuds.

He walked over to where the *Maria Louisa* sat still and silent on her wooden scaffold. He stared up at the ship's hull, its wood gleaming warmly in the sunlight. Above the hull was the deck, and above that, the masts with their complicated arrangements of sails.

The museum was filled with light. In addition to the huge wall of glass at the front, there was another glass wall at the side, and also a glass ceiling. Looking out the front, Lewis could see—just a stone's throw away down the slope—the Atlantic Ocean. It was so close to the ship that it was easy to imagine the *Maria Louisa* in her glory days, riding the high seas.

Another thud. Louder. It was coming from inside the ship.

"Crawley?" he whispered, feeling foolish.

The only voice that came back was Mrs. Sobowski's. "Davie, do you remember how we *act* in a museum?"

"Crawley?" whispered Lewis again. "Bellows? Adam?"

The next thud was strong enough to jolt the ship, and loud enough to catch the kindergartners' attention. A crash followed. Then a series of thuds.

Suddenly, a voice roared out, "You thinks you can *keep* our ship, does you? Through all eternity? Not while *I* carries a sword, you filth-ridden maggot! You weevil! You bucket of scum!"

Lewis looked around. The kindergartners were crowding into the exhibit hall, wide-eyed with delight. Mrs. Sobowski and the volunteers were smiling, too. They thought the voices came from actors. They thought this was part of a show.

There were yells now from the ship. Shrieks. More crashes. Mrs. Sobowski gave her class instructions that Lewis couldn't hear because of the noise. The kindergartners lined up behind her—and started moving toward the gangplank.

They were going on board!

"NO!" howled Lewis.

He launched himself like a missile, reaching the gangplank just ahead of the teacher. Blocking her entry, he shouted, "No! Don't! Please!"

The noise on the ship was growing louder, but Mrs. Sobowski's voice carried clearly. "*Excuse* me." She gave Lewis a look that would have flattened him under any other circumstances. "What's your name? Aren't you in Ms. Forsley's class?"

"You can't go on this ship!" Lewis spread his arms and grabbed the guide ropes.

Mrs. Sobowski pointed a stern finger. "*You* are getting yourself into serious trouble."

"I know," said Lewis. "But you can't go on."

A man in a museum uniform appeared. He was wearing a red clown nose, but he looked like he meant serious business. Seeing Lewis blocking the gangplank, he frowned and pushed past Mrs. Sobowski. "Step aside, son. Let—"

"No!" Lewis took a step backward, but held on to the ropes. "You can't!"

The man shook his head, as if he couldn't believe his ears. He reached for Lewis. "You come off there. Now!"

"No!" yelled Lewis, dancing backward up the gangplank.

From up on the ship came a bloodcurdling scream, followed by a string of curses. The kindergartners went, "Woooooo!" and clutched each other. The museum man glanced at the ship. Then he frowned again at Lewis.

Suddenly, there was a gasped "Ooohhhh!" from the kindergartners. Looking over his shoulder, Lewis saw the first pirates. There were two of them—Moyle and a stranger. They were dueling with swords up on deck. Moyle stood out in his lime-green Hawaiian shirt and white shorts.

A hand came down heavily on Lewis's wrist. It grabbed and held on. The museum man! He was pulling Lewis down the gangplank.

Lewis wrenched his arm free. He scrambled back up toward the ship. When his right knee buckled, he hardly paused. Just lurched to his feet and staggered on. He didn't stop till his path was blocked at the top—by a pair of worn black boots, streaked with sea salt. He looked up.

A tall cadaverous pirate, his eyes sunk into a skeletal face, barred Lewis's way. The stranger raised a blood-soaked sword. His mouth opened, exposing rotted stumps of teeth.

"Be you one of Crawley's men?" he cried.

If Lewis had stopped to think, he would have seen that there was a right answer and a wrong one.

"Yes!" he blurted.

Down came the sword! Right where his head should have been. Except that—reacting for the first time in his life at lightning speed—Lewis actually *saw* the sword coming and dodged it, darting under the pirate's arm onto the ship. Down in the crowd, someone screamed.

Lewis glanced back, expecting to be pursued. But the tall pirate was still at the gangplank, raising his sword again—this time against the museum man! Lewis dashed to the ship's railing. The museum man was crouched near the top of the gangplank, rigid with fear. The guide ropes trembled in his hands.

"Get off!" Lewis screamed at him. "Run!"

The museum man released the ropes. Scuttling sideways like a crab, he half-ran, half-fell off the gangplank.

Lewis turned to survey the deck. Everywhere, pirates were leaping and scrambling, swinging swords, flashing daggers. Pistols fired in explosive roars, raising clouds of pungent smoke. Bodies flew and smashed with noisy thuds against the wood. The deck shook. The sails trembled. The air was thick with curses and screams.

And Lewis was right in the middle! A bandy-legged pirate in rags ran at him, howling, sword in hand. In a flash, Lewis leaped sideways onto a sea chest. Bounding over a coil of rope, he skidded to the other side of the deck. Just ahead was Adam—no, Mary!—in a frenzied struggle with a bushy-bearded pirate twice her size. The pirate had his hands around Mary-Adam's neck. The cabin boy—girl!—swung wildly with both fists.

Lewis leaped onto the bearded pirate's back. His nose was assailed by a stench so foul, he could hardly breathe. Crawley was right. Up close, Dire's crew was rank! Lewis hung on, kicking and pounding till the pirate released Mary-Adam in order to claw at the boy on his back.

Mary-Adam, now free, dived at the pirate's legs. Whether she bit, punched or pulled, Lewis never knew, but the bearded ghost went down, taking Lewis with him. Scarcely had Lewis hit the deck, when a hand— Mary-Adam's—dragged him away.

"You mustn't fight, Lewis," shouted Mary-Adam in his ear. "You *mustn't!*"

"Why not?" Lewis was beginning to think he was doing quite well.

"Don't you see?" Her voice was pleading. "You're the only one of us who can truly get hurt. You could *die*, Lewis!"

Lewis looked around. She was right. He was the only one who wasn't already dead. The others could fight through all eternity, and they might experience pain—maybe they'd even lose more body parts—but the worst had already happened.

"Get yourself to safety," shouted Mary-Adam.

Lewis glanced back at the gangplank. The tall pirate was still guarding it, struggling now with . . . was that a policeman? Yes! Lewis could see the blue uniform clearly.

"This way!" begged Mary-Adam. "Shinny up the mainmast. You'll be safe there, in the crow's nest."

Lewis looked where she was pointing. Way up, at the top of the mast, almost at the ceiling, was a tiny platform.

Lewis's stomach churned. "I can't."

"You must!" said Mary-Adam. "Or you'll end up like us."

At that moment, they were both knocked flat by a flying pirate. Not actually *flying*, Lewis realized as he went down, just thrown across the deck. Stumbling slowly to his feet, Lewis tried to focus. Mary-Adam was up again, battling the flying pirate, and he, Lewis, was facing—

Captain Dire!

He could tell by the hair, a long, white mane flowing

261

down past the pirate's shoulders. But not just the hair. Crawley had described Dire well. That cold stare. Those bleak, blue eyes. That absence of all feeling. Lewis knew what he was looking at. Evil itself.

Slowly, Dire raised his sword till it was even with Lewis's chest. He looked relaxed, almost casual, as if finishing off Lewis would be a moment's work. Like squashing a wingless fly.

"Back off!" cried Lewis. He knew it was absurd, even as he said it. He was small, unarmed, inexperienced and most of all . . .

Alive!

Yes, that was it. He was the only one who was alive—and he was going to *stay* alive.

"Back!" he yelled again as the pirate came at him.

Slowly, deliberately, almost insultingly relaxed, Dire pulled back his sword—and thrust!

It pierced a cork float that Lewis had seized from the deck. He had moved so quickly and instinctively, he was hardly aware of the motion till it was over.

The sword stuck. Without waiting, Lewis dropped the cork, spun and sprinted across the deck. Reaching the mast, he seized the rope rigging and began to climb.

It was harder than it looked. He was wearing running shoes, and his feet slipped on the ropes so badly that soon he had to stop, expecting any second to feel

Dire's powerful grip on his ankles. Glancing down, he saw that Dire was indeed directly below. But he'd been cut off by Crawley, who yelled, "Stand fast and fight, bottom-feeder!"

Lewis took heart. Looping his left arm through the rigging, he used his right hand to pull off his shoes and socks. His bare feet, sweaty with fear and exertion, did a better job of clinging to the ropes. He ripped off the Frankenstein headpiece, too. His red hair sprung free as if released from prison.

Slowly, he climbed, telling himself, "One square, just one," then reaching for the next and saying again, "Just one." In this way, square by square of rope, he climbed the rigging. He didn't look down, knowing that a single glance would drain his courage like water from a sink. Another square. Another. Beneath him, the shouts and thuds continued. Were the kindergartners still in the hall?

Finally, he was there. Just beneath the platform. It took all his nerve and almost more strength than he had to curl his body over the top and flatten himself, like a sheet of paper, onto the small surface. Panting hard, he looked down.

He was instantly, terrifyingly dizzy. His stomach wobbled. Shutting his eyes, he took a deep breath. He looked again, willing his stomach to stay still.

Oh! He could see everything! It was like being a bird. *This* was why it was called the crow's nest.

Below, the battle raged. He scanned the deck fearfully, expecting to see Crawley's crew in retreat. But the more he saw, the more he realized that they were—somehow, improbably—hanging on. More than hanging on! They looked vibrant and bright now, colorful in their thrift store clothing, their skin glowing with excitement. Dire's pirates, in contrast, looked shadowy and gray. Their faces were sinister, their eyes cold and blank.

Lewis stared at his tower-mates, amazed. Here, Moyle fought a muscular rival, his cutlass flashing faster than Lewis could have imagined if he hadn't experienced his own surprising speed under pressure. There, Jonas held two ghosts at bay. His bare feet agile as a dancer's, he leaped from deck to rope to railing without a slip, his sword a sweeping, never-resting barrier. Jack, meanwhile, fought like the rodent he was named for. Seizing hard upon first this pirate, then that, he terrified them so badly they retreated to take on lesser foes. Even little Skittles held his own, hopping about in front of a lumbering tattooed brute.

But it was Barnaby Bellows who did the bulk of the fighting. He strode the decks like the giant that he was, and whenever he spotted a weakness—an enemy pirate distracted by one of his crewmates—he stepped in and with a single smooth, powerful movement, seized the scoundrel and hurled him over the side of the ship. Glancing around, Lewis could see five or six of Dire's men who'd been tossed overboard by Bellows. They were limping around the museum floor in various states of confusion.

Not surprisingly, the spectators had scattered. Lewis looked for Mrs. Sobowski and saw her, herding her students—or trying to—out the door. He could tell, even from here, that she understood the danger now and knew it was terrible and real. She was waving and yelling at the kids. The problem was that, in the great tumult of firing pistols and yelling men, the kindergartners couldn't—or wouldn't—hear her. As fast as she herded them out the door, they ran back in. Lewis could understand why. It was the kind of show they would never see again, not if they watched action movies for the rest of their lives! For Mrs. Sobowski, it was a losing battle, even with the help of the volunteer parents. There were just too many excited kindergartners. They were running free among the dazed pirates of Dire's crew.

Watching them, Lewis felt a stab of fear. If Dire's pirates posed a danger to him, what might they do to these kindergartners, scampering among them like rabbits in a lion's den?

And even if Dire's pirates didn't harm the children, they would certainly, once they got over their dazed state, reboard the ship. How long could Bellows continue to hurl them overboard? How long before they overpowered him and brought him down?

Suddenly, there was a brain-numbing blast of noise, followed by a great cloud of smoke. Lewis looked down. A *hole* had been blown through the museum wall behind the ship. Cannons! The pirates were now firing cannons! Screams came from a hysterical volunteer standing near the hole.

As Lewis glanced frantically from one peril to another, his worst fear came to pass. A kindergartner had managed to get up the gangplank and was standing on the ship's deck—right beside Captain Dire. It was *her*! The little girl with the red glasses! She was dancing with excitement at seeing the show so close. Lewis watched, helpless, as the pirate spotted her. Head thrown back, Dire laughed. He plucked the girl up with one hand and held her above his head, ready to hurl her overboard.

A sob escaped Lewis. Frantic, he searched the hall. Bellows was halfway down the gangplank, blocking Dire's men as they tried to reboard.

"Bellows!" screamed Lewis.

Everything stopped. For Lewis, it was like watching a movie that turns suddenly into a still photo. Everyone was staring up at *him*, Lewis. Mrs. Sobowski. Dire. The little girl, her mouth open in an O of terror. And most important—Bellows.

Lewis pointed. "There!"

Bellows's gaze shifted till he spotted the white-haired pirate, still gripping the wriggling girl. Captain Dire's arm reached backward. Like a football player, he prepared to throw . . .

Lewis watched it as if in slow motion. Bellows churned like a machine down the gangplank, flattening two of Dire's men on the way. Screaming, the little girl flew through the air, over the side of the *Maria Louisa*. Bellows ran, stopped, gauged his position, darted forward until—

He caught her like a football. Rolling backward, he held her ahead of him so she wouldn't hit the floor. She fell against his massive chest, which acted as a pillow as he went down with a mighty crash.

Up in the crow's nest, Lewis let out his breath with a cry. She was safe. And now the other kindergartners would leave.

But they didn't.

Watching, Lewis realized that they still thought it

was a game. The ones who had escaped Mrs. Sobowski were wild with excitement. They were crowding toward the gangplank, eager to be the next ones hurled by Dire.

Somebody had to stop it! Somebody had to *do* something. Lewis searched the deck. Where was Crawley? There! Lying next to the ship's wheel. Had he been knocked out? Who else might act? But all Crawley's men were once again engaged in their own battles. Nobody, except Lewis and Mrs. Sobowski, could see the danger.

With growing terror, he scanned the room—the deck, the floor, the exit corridor, even the ceiling. Then he looked through the window to the sea.

The sea.

He stared, as if hypnotized, at the gentle grass slope that ran down to the ocean. So close, so close. And he saw the answer! He saw it as clearly as a dream in the instant of waking. All that stood between the *Maria Louisa* and the sea was a thin sheet of glass and a short grassy slide. If the *Maria Louisa* went into the ocean, the pirates would follow.

All of them.

He had to do it. He, Lewis, had to command this ship.

He pulled himself to his feet and searched for the one pirate who could help.

"Bellows!" he screamed.

The giant looked up.

Lewis held out his right arm as commandingly as he could. Remembering the pirate books he had read, he yelled, "Prepare to launch ship. Bellows! Aft!"

Bellows stared back, uncomprehending. Lewis hauled up every shred of force in his being. With all his strength and spirit, he *willed* Bellows to understand.

"Aft!" he cried again. "Prepare to launch!" He pointed to the back of the ship.

Bellows wavered. Then, slowly, his huge face opened into a grin. His hand rose in a salute.

"Aye, aye," he shouted. He ran to the stern.

Lewis waited till Barnaby Bellows was in position at the back of the ship, ready to start pushing.

"Full ahead!" yelled Lewis from the crow's nest.

He couldn't see Bellows now, but he could picture him, his mighty shoulder tight against the *Maria Louisa*'s stern. Lewis could tell where Bellows was because of the groaning timber as the ship slowly shifted forward on her wooden scaffolding and then rocked back.

"Full ahead *again*!" yelled Lewis. "Barnaby! Now!"

The wood groaned again, then screeched. The ship shuddered forward toward the glass window. Then back. Then forward . . .

It was shifting! With the strength of a giant behind it, with the energy of a giant's two centuries of imprisonment, the ship was finally moving.

Lewis held tight as a barnacle to the mast as the *Maria Louisa* rocked and shook. The window loomed close—and still closer! He huddled down, his face buried in his jacket. One more surge and—

The glass shattered! Broken shards rained down on the sails, on the mast, on the crouched body of a clinging boy wearing a bright red jacket—a boy who looked, Lewis suddenly understood, exactly like the little sailor in the bottle at home.

He, Lewis, was that bright red sailor!

The *Maria Louisa* broke through on her journey to the sea.

And so did Lewis. In the moment of the crashing of the glass, something shattered in him as well. Walls he no longer needed, fences that had held his spirit back. They crashed with the glass, and he held on, eyes shut, as the ship surged forward—through the smashed window, past the broken glass, past the malevolent pirates, into the sunlight, into the wild raging wind.

28

The wind! It was like a living thing. It flew at Lewis, trying to hurl him off his perch. But he had fought too hard to be thrown off now. Wrapping both arms around the mast, he clung tight as the ship began a slow teetering slide down the lawn.

A cry rose from below as the *Maria Louisa* leaned to the right. Lewis swung right, too, his backside sliding along the platform. For a heart-stopping moment, his grip on the mast slipped. He seized hold with the desperation of the drowning. Pressing his face into the wood, he was still clinging when the ship somehow—a miracle!—righted itself.

No, not a miracle. Looking down, he saw that

Crawley's crew on the deck had scrambled as one to the opposite side, balancing the ship with their weight. And Bellows was still back there on the starboard side, pushing and straining with that astonishing unleashed strength.

The *Maria Louisa* groaned on down the grassy slope, pulled by gravity, pushed and balanced by human weight. Lewis glanced around. The last of Dire's pirates had been tossed overboard by Crawley's crew. They were running alongside now, looking for a chance to reboard. But Jonas guarded the railings with a small anchor tied to a rope. He swung it like a weapon, driving away any enemy who approached.

Abandoning the *Maria Louisa,* the gray-faced pirates ran for the replica boats instead. They swarmed like wasps over the Haida canoe and the Viking longship.

The *Maria Louisa*, meanwhile, swayed wildly down the last piece of lawn, her balance held only precariously by the shrieking pirates on deck and the giant pirate acting as a living rudder below. She was closing in fast on the ocean.

The grass ended with a jolt. The *Maria Louisa* dropped sickeningly over a small bank, causing the pirates on board to roll like bowling balls down the deck. Her prow hit the water with an immense splash. For a moment, Lewis was sure they would plunge straight to the ocean floor. But then her stern slid over the bank and splashed down too, throwing Lewis—and the pirates on deck—backward again. Rocking like a giant cradle, the *Maria Louisa* settled slowly into the waters she knew so well.

A whoop of triumph rose from the deck. They were launched! Up on his perch, Lewis started to join in, shouting and waving his right arm in circles like a rodeo rider. Then he happened to glance backward.

Bellows. He was still on shore! His task completed, he stood there, looking baffled and exhausted. Some of Dire's pirates were almost upon him. Others were dragging the replica boats, now torn loose from their moorings, down the grassy hill.

Lewis yelled at the crew below, but in all the racket, no one heard. He put two fingers in his mouth and let out a shrieking whistle. The pirates looked up. They saw Lewis point to shore, heard him shout Bellows's name.

Skittles was the first to reach a rope. In a blur of speed, he uncoiled it, tied it to a cork float and hurled it over the stern. It didn't even reach the shore. But on his next try—as the first enemy pirates leaped onto Bellows from behind—the float fell like a gift into the giant's hands. Bellows swung off the bank with his attackers still clinging and landed in the Atlantic with a splash.

Poor Skittles was dragged almost overboard by the weight. Just in time, Jack and Moyle joined him on the rope and held fast. In the water below, a furious Bellows thrashed like a breaching whale to throw off his pursuers. At last he was dragged, sodden and streaming, aboard ship. It took all of his crewmates to do it.

Another cheer rose up. Whooping, the pirates rushed Bellows to pummel and hug him and leap around his huge, soggy body. The joyous clamor thrilled Lewis to his bones. The *Maria Louisa* was theirs! It was launched—and Bellows had made it possible.

In the midst of the commotion, Bellows slowly raised an arm. He pointed up at Lewis, still perched in the crow's nest. The crew erupted again, louder than ever. But this time, they were cheering Lewis.

"LADDIE!" they yelled. "LADDIE! LADDIE!"

Mary-Adam began to climb the rigging. She was clutching a dark piece of cloth, and even in the wind, she was as nimble as a monkey. Within seconds, she was beside Lewis on the platform.

"You done a fine thing today," she said, her eyes filled with such feeling, she had to rub them with the back of her hand. "You're a true friend to us, Lewis. We never had better."

Then she held up the black cloth. A pirate's flag!

Not the skull and crossbones Lewis had seen in movies, but similar. This flag showed a whole skeleton, with a curved cutlass on each side. Balancing on the small platform, Mary-Adam tied the Jolly Roger to the mast. When it flapped open, there was another great shout from below.

As the cheer died, a powerful voice rang out. "Stand by to make sail!"

Crawley! He was finally on his feet. His gait was unsteady as he walked to the quarterdeck, but his voice was strong and clear. Responding to his command, the crew moved quickly to their posts. The deck came alive with activity as the long-imprisoned pirates remembered what it was to crew a ship.

Lewis glanced back to shore. The Viking ship and the Haida canoe were now at the water's edge, about to be launched by Dire's pirates.

"Look!" cried Lewis to Mary-Adam. "They're following. What if they catch up?"

The cabin girl shook her head. "Them boats look fine and new, but they ain't what that crew of scoundrels knows. It will not be easy for them, Lewis. See for yourself!"

Lewis looked more closely.

The Haida canoe replica was beautiful, but as he now noticed, it didn't have its paddles. The pirates who had claimed it were trying to steal oars from the Viking longboat—an effort that was being met by strong resistance from the pirates on the Viking ship.

"They're fighting each other!" muttered Lewis.

"Aye," said Mary-Adam, "and here we be—on the finest ship on the seven seas, on the grandest of all days. Can you feel these winds? Can you see these sails? Wait, Lewis, wait. You'll understand soon enough."

Lewis looked back to shore again. Behind the boats, the first of the kindergarten kids were now reaching the bank. They stood at the edge, waving, as Mrs. Sobowski ran to catch up. Two policemen stumbled along in the rear, one limping badly, the other punching numbers into his cell phone.

Mrs. Sobowski quickly shooed the kindergartners away from the water's edge. Then she turned to the ship. Her gaze moved up the mast. Shading her eyes, she stared straight at Lewis. Was that a smile?

"Will you come down now?" asked Mary-Adam in his ear. Her foot was on the rigging, ready to descend.

"Not yet," said Lewis. "I can see everything so clearly from here. I want to look a while longer."

The cabin girl grinned and slipped down onto the ropes.

As Lewis watched her descend, his attention was

caught by a series of angry shouts from below. He glanced around to locate their source.

There! From the hold of the ship, a pirate appeared, climbing up onto the deck. Lewis squinted. Not one of Crawley's men. Behind the pirate came Jack the Rat, shouting and wielding two swords.

"Lookee here!" yelled Jack. "See what I found below!"

It took Lewis a second to recognize the stranger.

Dire! It was Dire himself, his long white hair whipped by the wind, his pale eyes blinking in the sunlight. He must have still been aboard as the *Maria Louisa* started to move. He looked trapped now as he ran with a scarecrow clumsiness across the deck— searching, Lewis guessed, for a new weapon.

Before he could find one, Crawley charged. He bolted across the deck and seized his enemy by the scruff of the neck. Then he dragged Dire to the stern of the ship and slammed him—hard!—against the railing.

Jack the Rat followed, still clutching Dire's sword and his own.

Up in the crow's nest, Lewis held his breath. It would happen now, he was sure. Crawley's rage would finally erupt—the terrible, dark fury Lewis had witnessed for the past twenty-four hours.

What would it be? Keelhauling? The lash?

To his astonishment, he saw a smile on Crawley's face. A grim smile, to be sure, but one that was filled with intense satisfaction.

Facing the pirates on shore, Crawley hoisted his captive in triumph.

"Ahoy, ye sea scabs!" he yelled. "Does ye need another HAND? For yer OARS? For when ye has to ROW across the Atlantic?"

It was too windy, Lewis realized, for the crew on shore to hear. But seeing Crawley glance backward, he realized who the captain's *real* audience was—his own crew. They were howling as if this were the best joke they'd ever heard.

Crawley's next line got an even bigger laugh.

"I'd tie him up before I toss him over," he said, then paused for effect. "BUT HE AIN'T WORTH THE ROPE!"

And with that, Crawley seized his ancient enemy by the breeches and neck and tossed him, like garbage, over the rail.

The cheers that rang out on deck might have been heard on the other side of the ocean. They were certainly heard by the crew on shore. Lewis shouted, too, partly in relief. He hadn't really wanted to witness a keelhauling.

And then, as he watched Captain Crawley strut

away from the railing, his memory tossed up two words.

Gentleman Jim.

Of course, thought Lewis. It was just as McAlistair's book had said. Gentleman Jim.

Down on deck, meanwhile, Crawley's crew continued to holler.

"Drown, you bludger!"

"Down to the deep!"

"Send him to Davy Jones's locker!"

Crawley waited till the pirates had shouted their fill.

"Are ye done?" he asked finally, his smile filled with excitement and anticipation. "Are ye ready, mates? Can we make sail now?"

29

As the sails filled with wind, their snapping and billowing almost hypnotized the boy in red. Lewis couldn't stop watching. Slowly, with a magnificent grace, the *Maria Louisa* began to move.

At first, Lewis couldn't tell where they were heading, except away from shore. But gradually he noticed that the ship was traveling, not straight out to sea, as he had expected, but at an angle across the bay. Her speed increased by the second as she churned through the waves. Up in the crow's nest, it felt like flying. Lewis's clothing flattened against his body. His hair streamed behind him. The bright sunlight made his eyes squint, and the wind made his nose run. He had never felt so alive.

As the ship neared the other side of the bay, he was astonished to see people gathered along the shore. The cannons, he thought. The sound must have carried across the water, bringing people out of their houses and down to the bay. As the ship drew closer, he squinted, trying to see if the people on shore looked frightened, or maybe angry.

Mostly they looked . . . excited! Lewis gazed down at the *Maria Louisa*, trying to see it through the eyes of someone standing on shore. A boy like himself, for instance. What would the boy see? A ship full of pirates, that's what—in full sail, flying the Jolly Roger. Of course, that boy would be excited. He would be *wild* with excitement—and so would anyone else with a grain of adventure in his or her soul.

Lewis peered at the shore, trying to get his bearings. Tandy Bay looked so different from the water. He probably knew these buildings, but only from the front. He couldn't tell where he was until he saw the playground fence along the shoreline and the crowd of kids behind it.

Tandy Bay Elementary!

It must be recess. Every kid in the school, it seemed, had rushed to the water's edge to see the ship go by. Most were in costume, of course. They were gathered five or six deep along the wire fence, shifting and jostling for a better view. There were teachers watching, too.

Could they see him? Could they tell it was him? His hair was free now, and he was the only one in the school with hair that color.

Standing, he planted his bare feet firmly on the small platform. He gripped the mast tightly with his left arm and raised his right as high as it would go, waving it in a wide, slow arc.

"HEY!" he yelled, astonished at the strength of his voice, deeper and louder than it had ever sounded.

"IT'S ME!" he roared. "MEEE, LEWIS!"

On the shore, the kids stopped moving. They peered up at the crow's nest in disbelief.

"LEW—IS!" roared Lewis again.

The sound began slowly, then thundered back from hundreds of voices. "LEW—IS! LEW—IS! LEW—IS!"

He laughed out loud, standing even taller on the platform.

"LEW—IS! LEW—IS!"

He scanned the chanting crowd. Where was she?

There!

He could tell by the eye patch and the scarf tied backward over her hair. Abbie had *told* him she was dressing up as a pirate for Halloween. And there she was—halfway up the wire fence, a head above the others, waving her right arm in an arc that matched his.

"LEW—IS! LEW—IS!"

"ABBIE!" he yelled back, waving harder, hoping she would know he was waving at *her*.

In no time at all, the ship was past. Lewis gave his school a final salute before focusing again on the pirates as they scrambled with the sails. Then he glanced back toward the museum. As Mary-Adam had predicted, the Viking ship was far behind. The Haida canoe still drifted in the shallows.

Lewis climbed down the rigging the same way he'd climbed up, square by careful square. It was harder on a moving ship. The rigging swayed treacherously. But he moved with a new sureness now, a better understanding of what his body could do.

Down on deck, he was accepted as one of the crew. A few smacks on the back came his way, but mostly the pirates were busy with their work.

He looked where they were headed. The *Maria Louisa* was sailing across the bay again, and this time he recognized the shoreline. Shornoway stood out like a white beacon. He had never seen his house from the water before. It rose graciously from the cliff, a shabby but still elegant old lady. His heart warmed at the sight.

He focused on the tower, of course. As the ship sailed closer, he was surprised to see two tiny figures, like insects, in the tower's central window. He peered intently as they slowly became recognizable—his father and Mrs. Binchy. Excited, he waited to come closer still, but instead the *Maria Louisa* veered away. Looking down, Lewis noticed the bobbing buoys and beyond them, jagged rocks rising out of the sea. This was as close as the ship could come.

He waved. Would they recognize him? His father disappeared and returned a moment later, holding something to his face. Binoculars. Mr. Dearborn became suddenly very excited, waving and jumping up and down. He passed the binoculars to Mrs. Binchy, who started bouncing around too.

Lewis waved back with both arms. With his whole body!

"A grand old house," said Crawley behind him. "We was glad to have it all them years. How's your sea legs, lad?"

"Good," said Lewis. "I like it out here on the ocean. Things look different." His school had appeared much smaller. His house looked more beautiful and perfectly placed.

More than anything, he was amazed at the coincidence. On her journey out of the bay, the *Maria Louisa* had come close to shore only twice—and those two places just happened to be his school and his house. He mentioned this to Captain Crawley.

"Weren't no coincy-dence," said the pirate. "It were good sailing."

"You mean . . . you did it on purpose?"

"Aye. A chance to say good-bye, like."

"Good-bye?" A jolt, like electricity, ran through Lewis's body.

"Aye, lad. To your school. To your house. You're coming with us, ain't you?"

Seconds passed, during which Lewis could hardly breathe. He loved being here. Riding the *Maria Louisa*'s mast had been probably the best moment of his life. But . . . good-bye?

"Where are you going?"

Crawley smiled. "Ah, laddie. Do you have to ask?"

Lewis swallowed hard. His mouth could hardly form the word. "Libertalia?"

Crawley's good eye closed for a moment, and he breathed deeply. "Libertalia."

"But . . ." said Lewis, and for a moment that's all he could get out. "But is it real?"

"Real enough," said Crawley.

"I thought that Libertalia was like Neverland. Or Treasure Island. A story place. Made up."

"Ah, what's a story, lad?" said Crawley. "Life is a story. Your life is one. Mine's another. Libertalia? It's as real as . . ." He leaned in close to whisper, "You and me."

Lewis turned and stared at the horizon. They were almost out of the bay now.

The captain's voice in his ear was low and gentle. "They won't like it back there, you know—what you done today. Us sailing away in the *Maria Louisa*? There'll be the devil to pay for you, young Lewis, if you stay."

"I know," said Lewis.

"You're one of us now," murmured the captain. "You helped us take this ship. You'll swing for it, lad."

Lewis turned with a half-smile. "They don't hang pirates anymore, Captain Crawley."

The captain blinked. "They don't?"

Lewis shook his head. "Especially if they're eleven years old."

Gazing at the horizon, bright with the promise of adventure, he wondered what *would* await him back on land. Not hanging. But Crawley was right that Lewis would be in terrible trouble. He remembered the shattering of the museum window, and the policemen running red-faced down the lawn.

Then he remembered Mrs. Sobowski. She had seen.

She had understood. Lewis was pretty sure Mrs. Sobowski would be on his side.

"And my dad," he whispered. "And Mrs. Binchy. And Abbie. And . . . my mom, too, probably." He could think of others. In fact, there seemed to be a surprising number of people who might be on Lewis Dearborn's side back on land.

"Me and the boys," said Crawley after a moment, "we'd be proud as lords to have you on our crew. Why, seeing you run up those ropes—it done my heart good."

"It's my pirate blood," said Lewis.

Then, of course, he had to explain. Crawley was dumbfounded. He grabbed Lewis and hauled him around the deck, telling one pirate after another about Laughing Harry Douglas. They stared into Lewis's eyes as if he were the ghost of their long-lost shipmate, reincarnated and returned to take his place again on the crew.

"Aye," they said. "I see the likeness. I do! I do!"

Lewis couldn't imagine how there could be any family resemblance between him and Laughing Harry after so many generations. But something Bellows said made it clear.

"Aye," he agreed. "Harry were a bold 'un. Just like this lad here."

Crawley nodded. "That's what your great-granddaddy told us, young Lewis. I never believed him. But he were right!"

Lewis gazed back to shore. The *Maria Louisa* was moving farther out to sea with every moment. Shornoway grew smaller. As it shrunk, a feeling of profound longing came over Lewis, all the stronger because he wasn't quite sure what he longed for. The rocking of the great ship beneath his feet was a powerful thing. But Shornoway touched his heart.

Crawley was at his shoulder again, whispering, "Will you sail with us, lad? To Libertalia?"

Lewis stared hard at the white spot that was now Shornoway. He turned to Captain Crawley.

"I think," he said slowly, "I've already been there."

The pirate squinted back out of his one penetrating eye. "Aye, lad," he murmured. "I believes you have."

A yell rang out from the foredeck.

"There!" cried Moyle, pointing. "There on them rocks, straight ahead. That were where we foundered before. If we don't look smart, we'll do it again."

Crawley barked out orders. The crew raced to obey. Crawley turned to Lewis. "Can you make it back in a launch, lad?" He pointed at a rowboat. "We can lower one for you. Leastways, we can try. With the sea this rough, it'll be terrible risky. Can you hang on?"

Lewis nodded. "I'm good at hanging on."

He stared at the sea—a mass of heaving, roiling waves. They churned and broke against the ship's side. What would it be like in a tiny boat? What if the boat flipped, or smashed against the hull of the rolling ship? Could he swim to shore?

And what did such questions matter when there was no choice?

"I can make it," he said.

He turned to say good-bye to the crew. But they were rushing about, following Crawley's orders. Only the captain and Mary-Adam were near. The cabin girl darted forward. "I will miss you sorely, Lewis Dearborn. But you are choosing right."

He had to wait until enough crew was available to lower the rowboat. As he was about to climb in, Crawley spoke again, right into his ear, and Lewis was reminded of the first time he had heard that voice, in his brand-new room at Shornoway. It seemed like years ago.

"I won't say good-bye, lad. Just fare ye well. We never knows about fate. Me and the boys might sail these waters again."

Lewis gasped. "You might come back?" He couldn't help adding, "When?"

There was a long pause. Crawley grinned his gap-toothed grin. "Mayhap when you needs us again."

Lewis looked away so that the captain couldn't see his eyes fill. He climbed inside the little boat, then turned to Crawley.

"Or mayhap," he said, "when you needs *me* again."

Crawley roared with laughter. "Aye!" he cried. "We may have need of a lad such as you. Now go!"

The crew readied the rowboat quickly. Lewis crouched inside, holding tight to the sides as the little boat was raised off the deck, swinging from side to side.

"It ain't right," yelled Jack the Rat. "It's too rough. The laddie will drown!"

Lewis stared in surprise. The pirate's odd, angry face was contorted with alarm. Lewis couldn't believe it. Jack the Rat was *worried* about him.

"It's okay, Jack," he said. "Lower away!"

The rowboat rocked and banged against the ship's side—two, three, five times—as it went down, so hard Lewis was sure it would splinter to bits. He closed his eyes. Suddenly, with a stomach-churning drop, the boat fell into the ocean.

It hit the water so hard, Lewis flew forward, his chin ramming into a cross bench. It stung horribly, but that was nothing to the rush of freezing water that surged in as the boat tipped wildly to one side. Gasping, Lewis held on, leaning in the opposite direction.

Great-Granddad's face appeared in his mind, yelling something. Lewis couldn't tell what, but he knew it was encouraging.

He stayed low. He hung on.

The boat rocked again, once, twice, before reaching such equilibrium as was possible in the churning sea.

Lewis sat up straight. He shivered and looked around. The *Maria Louisa* was already far away. At her stern, Lewis could see the ghostly figures, growing smaller—Crawley, Mary-Adam, Jack.

He waved.

They waved back. Then they were gone.

Lewis sat for a moment. Then he put his hands on the oars. Swaying with the sea's movement, fingers icy, he looked backward over his shoulder toward land.

It was a long way. Shornoway was just a white spot with a tiny point for the tower. Lewis focused on that point. He began to row.

At first, it seemed impossible. The boat pitched and tossed, and his muscles screamed with the effort. But the incoming waves aided his struggles, and when he looked again, he could see tiny figures. Up in the tower window, the roundish figure of Mrs Binchy. Down on the beach, his father, wading knee-deep into the water to meet him.

They looked dear and important—but strange, too, like people he had known a long time ago. Hauling his boat through the sea, his arms sore and aching, he realized that he barely knew himself anymore. He felt as if he'd been on a long journey. The Shornoway that was waiting—and Tandy Bay, and Tandy Bay School—looked like different places from the places he'd left.

Better places, he thought. Happier places.

As he closed in on shore, he thought of Great-Granddad, feeling the old man's presence in the boat. He thought about the pirates, whose drowned bodies had washed ashore at exactly this place all those years ago.

Letting go of the oars, he turned in the boat to face his home. He leaned forward, smiling, as he allowed the waves to carry him in. He felt as if he was arriving on this shore for the very first time.

ACKNOWLEDGMENTS

Anyone who writes a pirate novel must rightfully thank Robert Louis Stevenson and J. M. Barrie for their enduring pirate characters and stories—bright beacons for the rest of us to follow.

Secondly, I'm very grateful to the BC Arts Council and Walter Quan for the writer's grant that got *Seven Dead Pirates* started.

Being a first reader of a novel manuscript can be a thankless task, so let me express my deepest appreciation for the comments of Deborah Hodge, Ellen McGinn, Norma Charles and Maurice Verkaar. Other writing pals who offered feedback and wisdom include Margriet Ruurs, Beryl Young, Susin Nielsen, Nan Gregory, Ellen Schwartz, Berny Lucas,

Ainslie Manson, Kathie Shoemaker, Andrea Spalding and Sheryl McFarlane.

How lucky can a gal get to have friends with lovely island homes who share them generously as writing retreats for a nautical tale? My heartfelt gratitude to Ellen McGinn, Susin Nielsen, Ainslie Manson and Margriet Ruurs.

I am lucky again to have a so-smart, so-passionate agent in Hilary McMahon. And lucky yet again with the amazing Tara Walker—editor, pal and sometimes even sailing advisor! Thank you, and thanks to copy-editor Jennifer Stokes, proofreader Shana Hayes and to the Tundra / Penguin Random House team—Terri Nimmo, Pamela Osti and Sylvia Chan.

Finally, and up close, I am always inspired by my daughters, Lia and Tess, whom I admire to no end, not least for their spirit of adventure. And to Maurice, a whole boatload of thanks—for naming most of the pirates in this book (Jack the Rat, gosh!) and for being such a generous, insightful listener.